You're So Last Summer

Sonia Palermo

Playlist

"Dear Maria, Count Me In" – All Time Low
"I'm Not Okay (I Promise)" – MCR
"I Miss You" – blink-182
"I Caught Fire" – The Used
"Ohio is for Lovers" – Hawthorne Heights
"You're So Last Summer" – Taking Back Sunday
"Thnks fr the Mmrs" – Fall Out Boy

For the full playlist, scan the code below or search "You're So Last Summer" on Spotify.

A Note From the Author

This book contains references to themes that may be distressing to some readers, including:

- Alcohol and substance use, including addiction

- Panic attacks and depictions of mental health struggles

- Pregnancy (briefly mentioned in the epilogue)

- Grief and sibling loss (motorbike accident, off-page)

While these themes are explored with care and empathy, your mental health and wellbeing are always the priority. Please take what you need and leave what you don't. If you're not in the right place for this story right now, that's okay—look after yourself first.

You matter.

And don't worry—this story *does* end in a happily ever after.

For Nonno,
who taught me to love beyond my means.

And for the elder emos, because we never
really got over it, did we?

1

GIA

This Could Be Anywhere in the World

T he air is always the same.

Spun sugar. Fried dough. The kind of sickly sweet that sticks to your hair and clings to your clothes. Memories on a stick, slowly going stale.

I walk the promenade, headphones in, ears bleeding nostalgia. Pastel shopfronts, sun-worn and faded. The slow buzz of half-interested tourists. That stretch of silence where Nico's voice used to be—the kind that never fades, no matter how loud the waves crash. No matter how many summers I try to outlive it.

I shake it off, blaming the ache in my chest on caffeine withdrawal. It's hard not to think about my brother when everything smells like him. Sounds like him. Feels like *then*.

As if I needed another reason to leave.

Up ahead, my PA, best friend, and all-around hype girl, Olive, waits outside Six. She's unmissable—a riot of colour and clashing prints. Her short, soft curls bounce in the breeze as she taps away on her phone, camera swinging against her chest.

When she looks up and spots me, her smile is soft. Kind. The way she always is first thing in the morning—for me, anyway. Olive is usually sunshine and sparkles before sunrise, but even she knows better than to hit me with full beam before coffee.

It's a small thing. But it matters.

The seagulls, though? Just one existential crisis after another.

And honestly? Same.

I pick up the pace. Just get through today. Just smile. Nod. Survive.

"You're late," she says, a half-smile tugging at her mouth.

I shrug. "Time's fake. Let's go."

She pulls open the door, and we step inside.

Cinnamon, citrus, and the sharp bite of espresso perfume the air around me. It's easy to like a place that smells this good. Easy to pretend I'm the kind of girl who belongs here. Warm lighting. Pretty plates. The curated ease of slow brunches and filtered selfies.

But I don't feel like *that* girl today. I feel like her shadow version—the one with walls up and a caffeine-shaped hole in her patience.

"It's cute," Olive says, surveying the room. "Cosy. Very grid-friendly."

A server leads us to a table along the outer wall. Just as well; I'm not in the mood to perform today.

We claim a corner spot—backs to the wall, eyes on everyone else. The place is already buzzing with the usual suspects: yummy mummies, aspiring influencers, out-of-towners, and hipsters in fisherman beanies.

Basically, it's the high school cafeteria—just with lattes and Botox.

"So?" she asks. "Last night's date? Give me something."

I sigh, flicking through the menu. "Predictably mid. Handsome, well-spoken, emotionally unavailable. You know, my type."

She grins, snapping a photo of sugar-dusted croissants as they float by. "One day, you're going to fall so hard you won't know what hit you."

"Doubt it."

Been there, done that. Zero out of ten. Wouldn't recommend.

Before she can protest, the server reappears. We rattle off our order like pros: plant-based everything, matcha lattes for the 'Gram, and a Vietnamese coffee for my rage.

And just like that, the conversation shifts—work, content ideas, the usual distractions.

Minutes later, the first round lands: vibrant açaí bowls, rose-coloured flat whites, French toast stacked with edible flowers, berries, and pistachio cream.

Instagram catnip.

Olive starts arranging the dishes for a flat lay. I lean in to adjust a napkin, and—

Shit.

The sleeve of my shirt catches the edge of the bowl. One second it's upright, the next it's all over me—purple, sticky, and fucking glacial. My jeans are soaked. My pride is bruised. My ego? Let's not even go there.

For a moment, all I can do is stare at it.

"Perfect," I mutter. "Exactly the vibe I was going for."

"You ate and left no crumbs with that one." Olive cackles.

I groan. "That's not even what that means."

"Doesn't matter. I'm still posting it."

I start blotting at the mess with a napkin, which does exactly nothing. "Kill me."

"Oh, absolutely not. We're milking this. Instagram vs. reality. *When brunch betrays you.*"

I open my mouth to argue, but Olive's gaze shifts—just over my shoulder.

Her grin softens into something sly.

"Well," she says, "if you want to borrow an apron, I think hot chef over there might be the answer to all your problems."

I follow her line of vision. The kitchen is open, buzzing with staff, but one guy stands out—tall, broad shoulders, sleeves rolled, a mass of dirty blonde waves...

Exactly my type.

He turns, and the world drops out from under me.

My stomach follows.

Of course it's him.

Of course it's fucking Charlie.

I go still. Cold.

My body reacts before my brain can catch up—heart in my throat, breath shallow, hands frozen around a soggy, purple-stained napkin.

No. Fucking. Way.

He's not supposed to be here. He's supposed to be on the other side of the planet, living the life he bolted for. Far away from this town. From me.

But it's him. Undeniably, unbelievably him.

Same smile. Same eyes. The boy I loved like gravity. The boy who left so easily.

"What the hell," I whisper.

"Gia?" Olive asks. "You okay?"

Not even slightly. But I don't let her see the way my hands won't stop shaking.

Charlie's eyes land on mine. He freezes. For a breath, it's just us—twelve years folding in on themselves, all the silence between us rising like a tide. The clatter of dishes, Olive's voice, the entire café—it all fades to static. Just me, him, and a decade of questions I never stopped asking.

Then he moves toward me, slow and careful.

"Gia," he says softly, his voice carrying a slight Aussie accent.

I cross my arms over my smoothie-stained front, holding the pieces of myself together with sheer will.

"What are you doing here?" I ask. The words come out sharp, clipped.

He rubs a hand over the back of his neck. "I—uh—work here. Guest chef for a while."

Guest. Right. Because he always leaves eventually.

I nod once. "Cool. Great. Love that for you."

There's a beat of silence. Then he gestures at my jeans. "You've got, uh…"

"Yeah. I noticed."

He smiles, almost sheepishly. "You always did know how to make an entrance."

I laugh once, dry as dust. "And you always knew when to disappear."

For a split second, his smile falters. I know I've hit a sore spot, but strangely, it doesn't feel as satisfying as I always imagined it would. All those years of fantasising about this moment, and now that it's real, the victory tastes... hollow.

"Relax, chef," I say, and it's a little mean. "It's a joke."

We both know it's not.

Then I look at him. Really look.

Not the way I did when I initially clocked him; the tattoos and the tight sleeves and that fucking hair. This time I take my time, make it obvious. Uncomfortable. Let him feel it. Mouth to eyes and back again.

He holds still like a man trying not to disturb a wild animal. I almost laugh.

Pathetic.

"How long are you here for?" I ask, arms crossed.

"Three months. Then back home to Melbourne. Makes a nice change to be back here, though."

Of course it's a *nice change*. Everything's a holiday when you leave the mess behind.

"Must be hell. Sunshine and therapy and people who journal," I say.

He tilts his head, watching me like I'm a recipe he can't quite decode. "What about you? Still live here?"

I shrug. "Someone's gotta keep the local wine bar in business." I shouldn't care that he knows nothing about my life now. But I do. "Still not forgiven, by the way." I keep it light, toss it out like it's casual. Like I haven't said those exact words a hundred times in my head—alone, in the shower, in dreams where he actually answers.

"For what?"

I don't answer. Because if I say it out loud—that he left, that he stayed gone, that he never said goodbye—I might not stop there.

"Ok, well good chat. Catch you around, chef."

He hesitates, like he wants to say something else. Like there's still time to fix this if he can just find the right words.

But he doesn't.

Instead, he gives a small, defeated nod and turns away. Walks back toward the kitchen like a kicked dog, hands shoved in his pockets, jaw tight.

I watch him go. Pretend I don't care. Then I sit down like nothing happened, even though my entire world just tilted sideways.

Olive stares at me like I've just spoken fluent Mandarin. "What was that?"

I blink, pleading ignorance. "What was what?"

She tilts her head. "You—him—that look. It was like I accidentally walked into the middle of a music video. A sad one. With rain. I couldn't figure out if you wanted to kiss him or mount his head on a plaque in your living room."

I shrug, taking a sip of lukewarm coffee. Suddenly I'm not hungry anymore. I say the first thing that comes to mind, something she might believe. Something that won't give me away. "Dunno. He just used to babysit me or whatever."

"What?" She almost chokes on her French toast.

"Yeah," I say, stabbing a strawberry with my fork. "My mum used to bribe him with leftover lasagne and Red

Bull. Very wholesome. Very Christian boy era. Now he's just... beardy and broody and accidentally hot, I guess."

"You knew him?"

I turn to her, throwing the fork onto the plate. "Knew is a strong word. He was my brother's best friend. Moved to Australia. Disappeared. Died or joined a cult or something. Now he's back. Cool story, huh?"

Olive narrows her eyes. "You're being weird."

"I'm always weird."

"Yeah, but like... emotionally constipated weird."

I smile sweetly, saying nothing.

She narrows her eyes further, then drops it—kind of. "Fine. But if this turns into some 'he was my brother's best friend and I loved him all along' saga, I'm telling everyone I called it first."

"Joke's on you. I don't love anyone. I barely love myself."

We both sip lukewarm lattes in silence for a second too long.

Then she side-eyes me. "You gonna stare at him some more or pretend he doesn't exist?"

"Depends," I say, scanning the crowd. "Is he still looking over here?"

She checks. "Nope. I think you scared him away."

"Good."

But it isn't good. None of this is.

I smile. Sip my drink. Play it cool.

But underneath? I'm a fucking wildfire.

Because he left. Because he's back. Because after all this time, one look still wrecks me.

2

CHARLIE

Reinventing The Wheel to Run Myself Over

"Christ. What a day," I mutter, kicking open the door of the beachfront shack I've been calling home. The salty air hits me like a slap and a hug all at once. I stand in the doorway for a second, just breathing it in. The crash of the waves is steady in the background, like some kind of promise that not everything falls apart. Some things just keep going.

I kick off my shoes, drop my helmet on the counter and my bag on the couch. The Boathouse has been my home for two weeks and I've yet to unpack. What's the point? It's all temporary. This gig. This place. Me.

I slide open the glass door and let the breeze flood the room, trying to loosen the knot in my chest. Out of habit, I dig into my pocket and pull out the little pouch of crystals I carry everywhere.

Yeah, I'm *that* guy.

But I'm also the guy who lost his best mate way too young. The guy who needed something to hold onto.

The black tourmaline's cool weight sits in my palm as I roll it between my fingers, grounding myself.

"Focus, Charlie," I whisper, closing my eyes. "You've got a kitchen to run. A life to rebuild."

But then—like clockwork—she flashes in my mind.

Gia.

She looked like a dream I'd been trying to forget. Like every half-memory I ever had of her got dragged through sunlight and sharp edges and made real again. Still gorgeous. Still sharp. Still the only girl who's ever managed to make me feel like I was standing on a trapdoor. And today? She pulled the lever and let me fall.

The purple-stained jeans. That blink-and-you'll-miss-it look of horror when she saw me. Like I'd crawled out of the past just to ruin her day. Or her life.

God, she flayed me. With her voice, her stare, that "get the fuck away from me" energy radiating off her like a furnace. I should've expected it. I did expect it. But it still got me.

She looked at me like leaving again wouldn't be fast enough.

I exhale hard, sinking into the old armchair by the window, the black tourmaline still clutched tight. My mind won't stop spinning.

I'd told myself there was no way we'd cross paths during my three-month stint here. She's got a whole life. What are the odds?

Apparently, shit odds.

And now I can't stop picturing her. That same casual kind of beautiful, like she doesn't even know. Like she could ruin you and not blink. And hell, she kind of already did.

I drop the stone into my lap, frustrated with myself. I reach for my phone, check the time even though I don't need to. Anything to distract me. Anything to stop myself from falling back into it.

She's not mine to miss.

I've watched her life from behind a screen for years. Sunshine, food festivals, all that curated joy. It looked perfect. Untouchable. But today? She looked like someone trying so hard to hold it together. Like maybe the cracks ran deeper than the surface. And that fucking gutted me.

Because I want to fix it.

Even if I don't deserve to.

I close my eyes, pinching the bridge of my nose. "Focus, mate." But her voice is still in my head. That edge. That venom.

She looked at me like I was the ghost she'd already buried. And now I've come back just to haunt her again.

I want to say something smart. Something clean. Like move on. But it rings hollow, even in my own mouth.

Because the truth is, I never really did.

I thought I could handle being back here. Thought I could handle seeing her again.

But after today?

Yeah. I'm screwed.

3

GIA

I'm Not Okay (I Promise)

I slam the front door behind me, the sound echoing through the apartment. Only then do I let it go. Rage crashes over me in waves. White-hot. Relentless.

Charlie.

Fucking Charlie.

It's been twelve years, and just like that—he's back. Like we pressed pause. Like he didn't fuck everything up.

How dare he?

Walking around like he owns the damn place, smelling of cinnamon buns and betrayal.

Who the hell does he think he is?

I storm into the living room and snap at Alexa to crank the volume. *Jagged Little Pill* blares through the speakers, and I start with "You Oughta Know", because obviously.

Alanis belts through the speakers while I stomp around, rage spilling out in sync with every lyric. It's not just seeing Charlie—it's everything. Every unresolved thing I thought I'd buried.

I shelved that book years ago. So why does it feel like I'm smack in the middle of the next chapter?

I hurl a cushion across the room. It lands with a sad, soft thud. Useless. Just like me.

The anger burns, but it's easier to sit with than sadness. At least it gets shit done. And I'm not about to sit here wallowing like wet lettuce.

I've been doing fine. Moving on. Building something out of the wreckage. And now he shows up, stirring it all up like no time has passed.

"Hand in My Pocket" kicks in. I drop onto the couch, burying my face in my hands. The tears don't come—just the white-hot, throbbing ache of everything I've been holding back.

Fuck him.

Fuck his fake accent.

Fuck the way he still smells like warm sugar and bad decisions.

I pick up my phone. Of course there's already a couple of texts from Olive. Girl's got a sixth sense for emotional spirals. Love that for her. Hate that for me.

> *Olive: You good??*

> *You dipped out fast*

Gia: Yeah

Just needed some air

Olive: Who was that guy?

You looked like you'd seen a ghost

Gia: Someone I'd rather forget

Technically not a lie. What am I supposed to say? "Oh, I laughed at his joke once." Like she'd buy that.

Olive: Oof

He didn't do anything, right?

Bc I can hate him on command. You know I'm petty.

Gia: Lol no

Don't hate him

He just… caught me off guard

And kinda broke me, but hey.

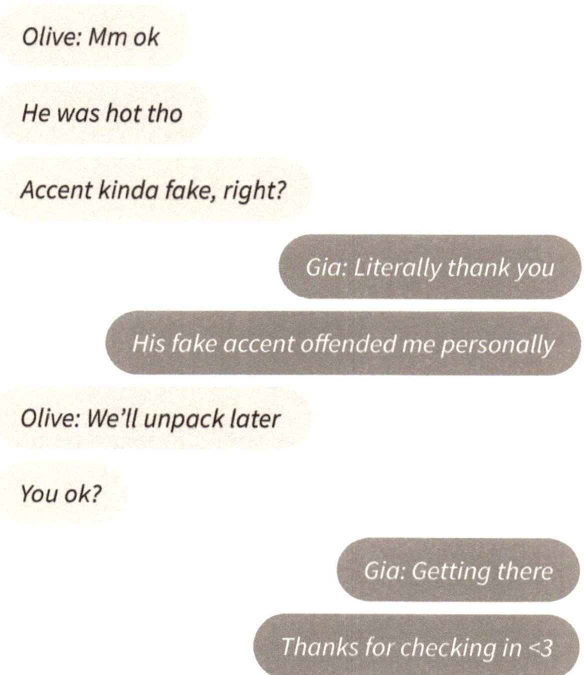

She always does. And I hate how much I need it. I want to tell her everything, but I'm not in the mindset to be splitting open old wounds just yet.

Olive: Shut up ILY more

I set down my phone and stare at the wreckage of my day. My stained jeans, the overturned cushion, the house still humming with unspent energy. I can't sit in this anymore. I need to move. To do something. Anything.

I peel off my clothes, trading them for a pair of running shorts and a sports bra. I pull on my running shoes. Tie my hair into a messy knot. Step outside.

The cool air hits like a slap—exactly what I need. The pavement's warm beneath my feet, and the sky is fading from blue to bruised pink. I take off down the street, each footfall pounding out the rhythm of *don't think, don't feel, just move.*

I push harder, faster—like I'm racing the horizon, like if I run fast enough, I can lap the past. Outpace the memories. Outrun the boy who became a ghost and then had the audacity to haunt me in broad daylight.

Olive's texts echo faintly in my mind, softening the edges just enough to keep me upright. She doesn't need the full story—not yet. But she sees me. She always has.

I hate how much that helps.

Of course Charlie is still hot. Of course he smells like baked goods and regret. Because the universe loves a sick joke.

My lungs burn, but I welcome the sting. Anything to drown out the echo of his voice. The way he looked at me like no time had passed. Like he hadn't broken everything and then left me to sweep up the pieces.

Just waltzing back in with that fake-as-hell accent and cinnamon-roll face, like it hasn't been twelve years. Like I haven't spent every one of them figuring out how to forget him.

With each step, the tension slowly begins to fade, replaced by a sense of release I haven't felt in days.

By the time I make it back home, I'm drenched in sweat and breathing hard, but it feels good.

I stand there for a moment, looking at the night sky, feeling the cool air on my skin, and for the first time today, the storm inside me calms.

At least for now.

4

CHARLIE

About A Girl

I'm up before my alarm. Not that it's surprising—I haven't slept well since I saw Gia. Christ. Even thinking her name messes with my head.

It feels like I've been thrown back twelve years, back to a time when things were easier and so much more complicated.

I drag myself out of bed, the cool air from the beach slipping through the cracks of the old shack. It's quiet here, just the sound of waves crashing against the shore, which usually calms me. But today, nothing is settling the noise in my head.

After a jog along the shoreline and a rushed cup of green tea, I decide to head into town. There's a farmers market in the village square every Saturday, and I figure a bit of distraction and some fresh produce won't hurt.

The market is already bustling when I arrive—stalls overflowing with fat tomatoes, crusty loaves of bread, beeswax candles and jars of honey. I'm halfway to the herb stall when I hear a voice that stops me in my tracks.

"Charlie?"

I turn around and see her—Mrs. Perelli, holding a canvas bag filled with lemons and fresh flowers. Her eyes widen when she spots me fully, and then her hand flies to her chest.

"Oh my god," she breathes. "It *is* you."

She pulls me into a hug before I can even process it. She smells like lavender and something familiar I can't name—home, maybe. Something I haven't felt in a long time.

When she pulls back, her eyes are already glistening.

"Sorry," she says with a quick laugh, dabbing at the corner of her eye with the sleeve of her cardigan. "You just caught me off guard."

"No need to apologise," I say quietly. "It's good to see you, Mrs. P."

"You too, sweetheart," she says, her voice thick now. "God, you look just like—" She trails off, clears her throat. "Well. Like yourself. But older. Wiser."

"Hopefully," I say with a weak smile.

She nods, but she's still blinking too fast. "It's been so long. Gia said you were back, but I didn't want to push. I didn't know if you'd want to see us. After everything."

There's a pause—just a beat too long—and I know what she means. After Nico.

"I've been keeping my head down," I admit. "Didn't expect to run into anyone. Let alone you."

She manages a smile. "Well, I'm glad you did."

She adjusts the strap of her bag, then tilts her head. "What are you doing tomorrow?"

"Tomorrow?"

"We're having Sunday dinner. Just us. Gia's coming. You should too."

I hesitate, the weight of her words sitting heavy on my chest. Sunday dinner at the Perelli's. A sacred ritual once. A reminder now.

She sees it. I know she does. And maybe that's why she reaches for my wrist and gives it a gentle squeeze.

"You were family once, Charlie," she says softly. "That doesn't just go away."

My throat feels tight. I nod, because I don't trust my voice not to crack.

"I'd love to," I finally manage.

She beams at me, teary and hopeful all at once. "One o'clock. Same as always."

As she walks away, I stand there for a long moment, the hum of the market fading behind the rush in my ears. My heart's beating too fast, and I already know tomorrow's going to mess me up one way or another.

5

GIA

There's No 'I' In Team

I pull up outside my mum's house, feeling the familiar comfort of the place settle around me. Sundays at Mum's have always been a constant—a time where the world can stay outside and everything feels... normal. And right now, I need that more than ever.

I step inside, kicking off my shoes by the door. "Mum, I'm here!" I call out, the warmth of the house and the scent of rosemary and crispy roasties welcoming me.

"In the kitchen, darling!" Mum's voice rings out, overly cheery.

I raise an eyebrow but shrug it off. She's probably just got some gossip she can't wait to share with me.

The house is as cosy as ever, filled with family photos and the mismatched furniture she's had forever. I wander into the kitchen, expecting to see her bustling around the stove, a glass of wine already in hand. But instead, she's setting the table, a little too meticulously for just the two of us. Then I notice the third place-setting.

"I thought Dad was working?"

"He is," she says without missing a beat.

I eye her suspiciously. "Mum? Who's coming?" I ask, trying to keep my tone casual but unable to ignore the sudden knot forming in my stomach.

"Oh, just someone I ran into the other day, she says, not meeting my eyes. "Thought it'd be nice to invite them over. It'll be fine, I promise."

I narrow my eyes. "Mum, please tell me—"

The sound of a knock at the door cuts me off.

"Oh! That'll be him!" Mum says brightly, wiping her hands on a towel. Before I can question her further, she rushes to the door, leaving me rooted to the spot, my heart hammering in my chest. It can't be—

The front door creaks open, and I hear the familiar low rumble of a voice that stops me cold.

No. Fucking. Way.

Not again.

I turn, my legs moving of their own accord, just in time to see him step inside, wearing that same cocky half-smile I haven't been able to shake from my thoughts all week.

Charlie. In my mum's house. For *our* Sunday dinner.

I feel the room shift, my heart skipping a beat as everything inside me screams in protest.

"Gia," he says, bright blue eyes locking on mine. His voice is soft, almost uncertain, but there's something else there too, like he's trying to gauge my reaction.

I stand frozen, the world tilting on its axis. My mouth opens to speak, but nothing comes out. I can feel my pulse in my ears, my chest, my fingertips. It's like I've been dropped into some kind of sick, cosmic joke, and I'm not in on the punchline.

"Oh, look at you two! Isn't this nice?" Mum chirps, completely oblivious to the tension practically vibrating off me. "Sit, sit! Dinner's almost ready. What would you like to drink, Charlie? We have wine, beer, juice..."

"Water's fine. Thanks, Mrs P."

I can't move. Can't breathe. My legs feel like lead as Charlie takes a step forward, his presence filling the room in a way that's all too familiar.

I swallow hard, forcing myself to find my voice, though it comes out hoarse. "You... you didn't tell me he was coming."

Mum frowns, glancing between us like we're the ones being strange. "What's the big deal? You two were always close, weren't you?"

Close? Close doesn't even begin to cover it.

Charlie's eyes haven't left me since he walked in, but I can't bring myself to meet them. Not fully. Not yet. My fists clench at my sides as the memories of last week, of twelve years ago, swirl in my head.

"Yeah. Real close," I mutter, more to myself than to anyone else.

"Mm, something smells good," Charlie says, glancing around the kitchen.

Mum beams at him, clearly pleased. "We've got jackfruit turkey if that's okay? I hope you like your veggies—you always did."

I watch Charlie's face as he nods, a faint smile playing on his lips. It feels so familiar, and yet, it sends a jolt of irritation through me.

"Always were an advocate for the animals and the strays," he says softly, eyes flicking toward her. "Me included."

Ass-*kisser*, I think, resisting the urge to roll my eyes.

"Where's Mr. P?" Charlie asks, looking around as if my dad might suddenly appear.

"Working as usual," Mum replies, busying herself with the table settings.

"Right," Charlie says, his gaze flicking back to me. "So it's just us, then."

"Just us," I repeat, my heart racing as I realise how loaded those words are.

Mum sets a glass of water in front of him, her smile bright. "Are you sure you don't want something stronger?"

He shakes his head, casual confidence in his voice. "No, I'm good. I don't drink."

My heart does a little flip, and I can't help the smirk that pulls at my lips. "More for me, then." I pour myself a large glass of wine, relishing the cool rush of it hitting the glass, anything to distract from the tension thickening the air.

Mum raises an eyebrow at me, but I ignore her, lifting my glass to take a generous sip. The wine hits my senses like a comforting wave, and I glance at Charlie, who's watching me with an expression I can't quite read. It's a mix of amusement and something deeper, and I quickly look away, feeling the heat rise in my cheeks.

"Guess I'll be your designated driver," he says with a light chuckle, trying to ease the awkwardness, but it only adds to the tension swirling around us.

"Aw, how noble. But I'll risk the walk—it's not like you haven't left me stranded before."

Charlie flinches—barely—but I catch it. His mouth opens like he might say something, then closes again.

Mum interjects, her voice cheery. "Let's focus on dinner! I can't wait for you two to catch up."

Right, dinner. Just a casual family meal. Nothing weird about that at all.

"I'll be right back," I say, pushing back my chair.

I don't wait for a response as I head upstairs, toward Nico's old bedroom.

As I walk, I can feel the wine settling in, making my steps a little unsteady. I should've known better—wine never agrees with me. But maybe that's what I need right now. A little softness. A little blur. A chance to breathe away from the awkwardness and memories thick in the air.

Nobody will follow me in here. They never do.

I've been slipping into Nico's room for years, on and off. Everything's still the same. Like a snapshot from a noughties teen movie. Posters of My Chemical Romance, Blink-182, Nirvana—faded, curling at the corners. His guitar leans in the corner, dust softening the strings. Silent. Like him.

I pull open the desk drawer and there it is—his old phone. A fossil. I smile at the thought of him texting friends at 1 a.m., swapping jokes and half-finished lyrics.

The shoebox under the bed is exactly where I left it. My knees press into the carpet as I pull it out, already knowing what's inside: photos, torn ticket stubs, scraps of memory. All of it worn from being held too often.

I just want to feel him again.

Nico always knew what to say. Even when we clashed—me cynical, him endlessly optimistic—he could find light in everything. He believed in silver linings. And maybe I believed in him enough to pretend I saw them too.

I pick up a photo from one of our birthdays. He's grinning at the camera, arms around me, both of us smeared with cake. The edges are frayed, dog-eared. Familiar. Next to it, there's a postcard of Rome, the Trevi Fountain captured in that cheap, glossy way, a memory from one of our trips as kids. We'd tried to toss coins over our shoulders, giggling as they splashed, him promising we'd come back when we were older, when we could do it all properly. I close my eyes and pretend I'm still in that moment. Still his little sister, with a whole life untouched by grief.

My hand grazes something else—another photo. This one of him and Charlie. A festival selfie. Arms slung over shoulders, sunglasses hiding bloodshot eyes, their faces wild with joy. I can almost hear the music, feel the chaos vibrating off the image. A different kind of intimacy.

My heart squeezes.

The laughter, the crush I tried to bury, the heat of being young and invincible—it all floods back. All the feelings I stuffed into a box like this one, hoping time would erase them. It didn't.

Tucked in the corner, I find a tiny stash of weed. I pocket it without thinking. A tribute. Something to hold onto.

I sit back on the floor, the photo still in my hand. And for a moment, it's just me and them. Nico and Charlie. Two halves of a past I can't outrun.

I thought I'd locked this all away.

But memories don't stay buried.

And feelings? They don't, either.

6

GIA

Ohio Is for Lovers

By the time I crash out at home, I'm still carrying it all—Charlie's voice echoing in my ears, the heat of his gaze, the ache in my chest I keep pretending isn't there.

I curl up on the couch, Nico's little bag of weed tucked beside me like some fragile secret, and scroll aimlessly through my phone until Olive calls.

"Okay," she says, cutting right to it. "Spill.'

I exhale slowly, dragging a hand through my hair. "Dinner was fine. Until Charlie showed up."

There's a beat of silence. "The chef?"

I close my eyes. "The chef who ran off to Australia after Nico's funeral and never even said goodbye? Yeah. That Charlie."

"What the fuck?"

"Yeah. That about covers it."

She lets out a dramatic gasp. "I knew it. How?! Why?! Tell me everything."

I stand and start pacing. "Apparently he ran into Mum at the market. She invited him for dinner, like it was totally normal. Like he didn't just... vanish."

Olive's voice softens. "Babe... are you okay?"

"No. Not really." I press my hand against my chest, like I can slow the storm. "We sat across from each other like strangers. He talked about his life in Australia. I talked about work. And Mum just... filled in the gaps. It almost felt normal, which made it worse."

She's quiet for a moment. "Did he say why he left? Why he didn't say goodbye?"

I sink back onto the couch, staring up at the ceiling. "Not really. I didn't give him the chance. I was too busy pretending I didn't feel like my ribs were caving in every time he looked at me."

"Oh, Gia..." Her voice is gentle now, grounding. "You've been carrying that shit around for years."

"I know." I locked it away. Buried it with everything else I couldn't face. "I'm sorry I never told you about him." My voice catches, but I push through. "Anyway, then Dad came home, and he nearly cried seeing Charlie. They used to be so close, Ols. Like real father and son. And I just—snapped. I had to get out."

"You're allowed to be angry."

"I don't even know what I feel. Grief. Rage. Guilt. He got to leave. Got to live his life. And I stayed here, stuck in the wreckage."

There's a pause, a breath between us.

"Except now he's back," Olive says. "And maybe… not everything's wrecked."

I scoff. "Don't go getting all poetic on me.'

"I'm just saying. Dinner might've been a trainwreck, but maybe it's time for a redo."

I groan. "Don't say it."

"Let's go back to Six. You barely even ate. We'll get properly stuffed this time—maybe even literally, if you play your cards right."

"There it is," I mutter, but I'm smiling despite myself. "I'm not seeking him out."

"Nooo, of course not," she teases. "Total coincidence if we just happen to get a table when he's working again."

"I can't anyway. I've got that sponsored Q&A at the food festival. Need to test recipes, edit my content, pretend I know what I'm doing."

"Boring. But fine."

"I also kind of need a break from eating out, honestly. My mum still thinks I live off instant noodles despite the fact I literally get paid to eat."

"The irony."

"Right?" I sit back down. "Let's wait a week. I don't want to look like a stalker. Not that there's anything to stalk. It's not like this is… anything."

Olive makes a delighted noise. "Oooh, the denial is strong with this one."

"Stop."

"I bet he has a food kink."

"What?"

"Like… gets off watching people eat, or cook. Maybe he likes to get real messy…"

"Olive—"

"Come on, picture it. Charlie. Shirtless. Covered in flour."

"Oh my god—"

"Kneading dough. Sweat dripping from those sexy forearms. Moaning about soufflés and coq au vin..."

"I hate you."

"You're welcome, slut," she cackles. "Anyway, I gotta run. Late for yoga."

"Namaste, bitch."

"Love you."

"Love you too."

The call ends, and the quiet returns.

I stare at the phone in my hand, the screen fading to black.

Still holding on.

Still not sure how to let go—or let him back in.

7

CHARLIE

Buried Myself Alive

I don't do days off like this often. Rare Saturdays where I can wander without a schedule, no apron, no orders. But here I am—at the food festival, soaking in the noise, the smells, the chaos.

And of course, my mind won't shut up about one thing. Gia.

Every damn thought circles back to her. Every waking moment I'm stalking her Insta like a creep, hovering over the message button like some lovesick puppy.

Maybe I'm chasing a ghost, but if there's a chance—any chance—I'll find her here today, I'm gonna take it.

The crowd is thick, the air sticky with heat. The scent of fire and sweet fried dough swirling around me. I'm halfway through a brisket sandwich when I see her, laughing and joking with her chaotic bestie.

The sun catches her hair just right—dark and glossy, swinging over her shoulders the same way it did the night I first saw her across that grimy emo gig. Back when I didn't know her name, but already knew I was in trouble.

Something shifts in my chest. Might be the heat. Might be the hunger. Might just be her. Either way, my heart kicks up, way harder than it should.

I'm just about to make a move when Olive spots me. She says something, nudging Gia. And then—our eyes lock.

My breath stumbles.

Fuck.

My cock twitches like a fuckin' traitor. Literally salivating. Christ. Behave.

I school my face, aim for casual. But inside? I'm a fucking wreck.

"Hey," I say, settling on the bench next to them.

"Hey." Her nonchalance is fucking torture.

Olive grins like she knows something I don't—and she's enjoying keeping it to herself.

"How's it going, girls?" I ask.

Girls? What are you? Twelve?

I barely get the chance to say more before a voice calls out, "Gia! Your Q&A's starting."

She glances at me, then back to Olive. "Be right back."

The wind's knocked out of me the second she stands. White crop top, tiny denim shorts, legs for days—even if she's barely scraping average height. Doesn't matter. She looks like a goddamn knockout.

Then she's gone—mic in hand, slipping under the canvas of the demo tent like she's got a job to do and no time for me.

Way too optimistic of me to think we'd be on some kind of amicable level after the other day. Nope. Looks like I'm right back to square one.

Olive nudges me, a sly smile playing at her lips. "Come on, let's go."

She stands, heading toward the tent without waiting for a reply. I swallow and follow, trying to keep my cool even though my heart's pounding.

The crowd gathers as Gia's name is announced, the air thick with a quiet kind of electricity.

And suddenly, Gia the influencer takes the stage. She's like a different person.

Public speaking is totally her thing—natural, easy, warm. She chats about recipes, favourite comfort foods, even the weirdest dish she's ever dared to try.

You'd never guess she's got a chip on her shoulder. Maybe I'm the only one she can't stand.

I watch her, and damn—I'm impressed, scared, and turned-on, all at the same time. I don't know if it's the way she bites her lip when she's thinking, or how she shifts her weight from foot to foot, but there's something magnetic about her. The whole space seems to lean in.

And for a moment, I forget I'm just some bloke on the edge of the crowd, watching the woman I can't stop thinking about.

Olive sidles up beside me. "So, what's the plan, chef?" she asks, voice light, eyes sharp.

I raise a brow. "Plan?"

"You know... with her."

"I've got no idea what you're talking about."

She scoffs. "Well... are you gonna be the guy who makes her smile... or the one who breaks her heart again?"

My grin falters. The air shifts.

I meet her gaze, and beneath the smirk, there's steel. Something serious.

"I'm here for the good stuff," I say—quieter, more honest than I meant it to come out.

She doesn't blink. Just holds my gaze a beat longer than I expect. Then she nods.

"Good," she says. "Because if you screw this up, you'll have me to answer to."

I huff a laugh, trying to play it off, but her words bury deep. Lodging somewhere in my chest, in that space where doubt lives. Because she means it. And I don't want to fuck this up.

When Gia finishes, she strides over, cheeks flushed, eyes bright.

I want to tell her how good she was, but all I manage is a goofy grin.

"You did amazing," Olive says, pulling her into a hug.

"You really did. You were... incredible," I finally get out.

"Thanks," Gia says, and for a second, I swear there's something there—a flicker, a glimmer—something I can hold onto. Maybe she doesn't hate me as much as I thought.

"So, G," Olive jumps in, eyes sparkling, "I've been thinking about how you can boost your engagement..."

Gia looks at her, unsure—as if it could go either way.

"How about you and Charlie do a live? It'd be great content."

I raise a brow, smirking. "A live, huh? You really think people wanna watch me boil potatoes?"

Gia blinks, her smile faltering. She doesn't have to say anything for me to know she's completely against spending any more time with me.

Ouch.

But I know Olive's game—and I'm not opposed to it. The fact that Gia's best friend is giving me a chance to prove myself fires me up.

Olive snorts, rolling her eyes. "Not potatoes, genius. You know, something sexy."

"Something sexy, huh?" I shoot Gia a teasing look, and her cheeks flush. I can't fucking help myself. "You really think I can pull off sexy, G?"

I don't miss the way Gia's cheeks redden at my comment, just before she quickly schools her expression into something serious and annoyed.

"Wait—Ols, what exactly are you thinking?" Her voice has that sharp edge I know too well—the one she uses when she's caught off guard but doesn't want to show it. Her eyes flick between Olive and me, trying to suss out if this is a joke or some kind of setup.

Olive leans forward, eyes flicking between us. "I'm thinking something more... intimate. Like in your home kitchen, Charlie, if that's cool with you. Feels way more personal—better content for Gia's followers. Good exposure for Six, plus," she shrugs like it's no big deal, "people love the flirty, behind-the-scenes stuff."

Gia shoots Olive a look that screams *What the fuck are you doing to me?* "Behind-the-scenes flirty stuff?" she repeats, like the words taste sour in her mouth.

Shit.

I open my mouth, ready to crack a joke, but nothing comes out fast enough.

Olive, totally unfazed, presses on. "Come on, G. You two have chemistry. It's obvious. People eat that shit up."

Gia doesn't laugh. Doesn't move. Just stares.

"Look," I cut in, palms lifted in mock surrender. "It doesn't have to be anything you're not cool with. We can keep it totally PG. Make soup, or oatmeal. Talk about spice levels. Real wholesome content." My voice is too fast, too eager. "It's really not that deep, G. Just some fun kitchen stuff."

Fuck, reel it in.

Gia finally turns to me, and her expression softens—slightly—but it's guarded. "You think this is funny?" she asks.

"No," I say, honest now. "Not funny. I just... I like the idea of cooking with you. That's all."

Silence hangs between us for a beat too long.

Then she sighs, rubbing the back of her neck. "I don't know, guys. My followers already think I'm doing some kind of slow-burn fake dating thing with that sourdough guy from Manchester. They're barely surviving that."

I laugh—too loud, too forced. *Sourdough guy?*

Cool.

Real cool.

"Wait—that TikTok thirst trap bread bro? The one who fingerbangs his focaccia?" I ask, aiming for casual and missing by a mile. "What's his name—Jason? James?"

"Jake," Gia says, not quite meeting my eyes.

Right. Jake.

Jake the fucking sourdough violator.

I nod, stuffing my hands into my pockets before I do something ridiculous like fold my arms or cross them over my chest like a jealous teenager. "Well, I bake bread too," I mutter, then immediately want to punch myself in the face.

Olive snorts. "Jesus, mate."

Gia lifts an eyebrow. "You bake?"

"Are you kidding?" I say defensively, like I'm on trial. "My fermented rye is critically acclaimed."

Her lips twitch, and for a second, the tension breaks. "Right. I'm sure it is."

I shrug, recovering. "Point is, you've got options, G. Bread guys. Potato guys. Sexy off-menu chaos chefs. Whatever you need."

That earns me a real laugh, and my chest eases a fraction.

She eyes me for a beat. "Fine. But if I step foot in your kitchen and you so much as wink at the camera like you're on *MasterChef: After Dark*, I'm walking."

I smirk. "No winking. Got it. Just serious culinary professionalism… and maybe one apron-only shot for the grid."

Olive groans. "You two are exhausting."

Gia shakes her head, but she's smiling now—really smiling. "You better clean your countertops, chef."

"I'll even mop," I say, mock-solemn. "Only the best for my guest star."

Gia looks wide-eyed, caught between fleeing and agreeing.

"Ols…" she starts, but Olive grins, cutting her off.

"Come on, G. It's fresh content. Intimate. Sexy chef's kitchen vibes. Perfect for your feed. People eat up behind-the-scenes stuff. It'll boost your brand."

Gia exhales, stiffening. Her eyes flick to Olive, then me, still scanning for reasons to say no.

I lean in, voice low and teasing. "It's just a kitchen, G. I promise I won't burn it down."

Her eyes catch mine, and the teasing shifts—something real flickers between us. She swallows, then nods. "Okay. Let's do it."

Olive claps, grinning like she's won a prize.

I straighten, heart thudding. My kitchen. Her, in my space. The thought sets my pulse racing, my mind spinning with what could come next.

"Monday work?" I ask.

"Perfect," Olive says.

Gia bites her lip, glances at me with a spark of something mischievous. "See you Monday."

They walk off, and I'm left grinning like some lovesick cunt. A live cookalong. Me, cooking with Gia—and all her followers. Wild.

But maybe just the kind of wild I need.

8

CHARLIE

Sugar, We're Goin' Down

I 've done a lot of things in kitchens, but going live on social media? That's a new one. And doing it with Gia standing right next to me? Christ. My palms are slick, my heart's racing, my cock is stirring.

Breathing deep does nothing. My thoughts spiral—Gia in my kitchen, laughing at my terrible jokes, leaning against the counter... just the two of us, close enough to touch.

I swallow hard, willing my body to calm down, but it's impossible. The thought has taken root, growing, spreading through me like wildfire. Not even black tourmaline can save me now.

Three shirt changes later, I settle on a red plaid overshirt with a white tee underneath. Classic. Casual.

Wholesome chef trying to win back the girl of his dreams vibes—no pressure.

In the kitchen reflection, I catch myself adjusting my cuffs for the hundredth time. This was a bad idea. I'm way out of my comfort zone. But it's hard to say no when Gia's involved.

I hear a knock and swallow hard. Right. It's just Gia. No big deal.

But when I open the door, the sight of her makes me freeze. She's wearing the exact same outfit—red plaid overshirt, cropped white tee. Those tiny denim shorts again. She raises an eyebrow, her mouth twitching like she's trying not to react. Guarded. Measuring me.

I blink, then laugh, a little nervously.

"Wow," I say, gesturing to her. "I didn't realise we were doing matching outfits today."

She glances down at herself, her smile faltering for a split second before she laughs along. "Oh my god. We're like one of those cringey couples."

I'm about to brush it off with a joke, but something in her voice makes me pause. She's joking, yeah—but also maybe a little horrified. And if she's embarrassed, there's no way I'm letting it stick.

"Okay, wait," I say, holding up a hand. "Give me one minute. I can't—nope. We're not doing this. Not on camera."

Her brows lift in confusion, but I'm already backing toward my room, muttering something about outfit changes and damage control.

Before she can protest, I dart back to my bedroom and tear through my closet, yanking off the plaid and swapping it for a simple grey Henley. Still casual, a little more put-together. I exhale, already feeling more like myself.

When I come back out, Gia's perched at the kitchen counter, watching me with an amused expression. "Really? A Henley?" she says, raising an eyebrow. "Trying to be the next Sourdough Guy?"

I grin, leaning one hand on the counter, a little closer than before. "Don't worry—I won't be sticking my fingers in any of the food. Unless you ask nicely."

Her brows lift, and for a second, she looks like she might actually smile—until her gaze dips, just briefly, to my mouth. She catches herself almost instantly, rolls her eyes instead.

Smooth, Charlie. Real smooth.

She straightens, pushing off the counter. 'So, what are we making, anyway?" she asks, all business now—but her voice is a touch lighter, her eyes still holding the edge of a smile she's trying hard not to show.

"Jaffa cakes," I say, "with a twist."

"I'm listening…" Her tone is cautious, like she's bracing herself for something weird.

"It's kind of a hear-me-out dish," I say, trying to sound confident but knowing it sounds ridiculous.

We move over to the kitchen setup. I lift the lid off a bowl, revealing a glistening pile of jelly ears soaking in orange juice, the citrus scent sharp and slightly tangy.

"What are those?" she asks, her nose scrunching in disgust.

"Jelly ears." I shrug like it's no big deal, but I catch the hesitation in her eyes.

"It's a kind of mushroom, actually. Weird texture, but surprisingly good once you get past the look." I grin. "And they soak up the orange juice like a sponge. Adds a bit of a zing."

Zing? Christ.

Her lips press into a thin line, clearly fighting the urge to recoil.

"They look a little gnarly, I know. But give them a chance," I say, half-joking, half-serious.

I'm not sure if I'm talking about the jelly ears... or myself.

She tilts her head, then deadpans. "Okay, chef. Let's see what you've got."

I launch into the rundown—ingredients, the lore, the plan—starting simple with a vegan sponge. Gia's already got the live stream running on her phone, comments flying in like fireworks.

She's good at this. Effortless. Laughing, chatting with her followers like she was born holding a ring light.

Me? My palms are sweating, and my brain's juggling recipe steps and how not to come off completely awkward on camera.

"So, we're using jelly ears for the jaffa part," I say, whisking ingredients. "Also known as Judas' ear mushrooms. Bit of a weird name, I know, but there's a story behind it."

Gia throws me a sideways glance, one brow raised. "Isn't it because they grow on elder trees, and Judas—y'know, *the* Judas—supposedly hanged himself from one?"

I nod, impressed despite myself. "Exactly. Bit grim, but there's something kind of fascinating about using an ingredient with that much history."

She smirks and leans back against the counter, arms folded. I'm halfway through explaining how the mushrooms got their name—like, actual Biblical Judas—when she flashes a sly smile at the camera.

"Fitting," she says casually. "You've definitely got a bit of a Judas vibe, chef."

I pause, raising an eyebrow. "Betrayer of Christ? Bit harsh, no?"

She shrugs, still smiling for the stream. "I mean, he did kiss Jesus and then disappear for a while, didn't he?"

The comments explode with laughter and thinly veiled innuendos. Gia doesn't elaborate. But I catch the glint in her eye. She wasn't just talking about the mushrooms.

I stop whisking for half a second, the sting of her words softened only by the teasing glint in her eye.

"Wow," I say, half-laughing, half-flinching. "Coming in hot with the biblical shade."

"Just saying," she says with a shrug, all innocence. "If the mushroom fits..."

I shake my head, smiling despite myself, and focus on the batter, while Gia reels off some of the comments;

"Did she just call him Judas?? I'm screaming"

"omg the tension. do they hate each other or want to kiss???"

"@giaeats please blink twice if this is your situationship"

She's having way too much fun with those.

Me? I don't even know how to feel. Embarrassed? Flattered? Like I've just been roasted on live video by the girl I ghosted then couldn't stop thinking about?

Yeah. That.

I pour the batter into the tin and slide it into the oven, trying to stay cool. "This should be a quick bake, and then we'll top them with the jelly ear mushrooms and, finally, the chocolate."

Gia turns back to her phone. "Okay, let's hear it for our chef—questions for Charlie, go!"

The comment section lights up like a Christmas tree.

"@giaeats is he single??"

"how do you two know each other"

"how tall is he? blink twice if 6ft+"

"GOD THE TENSION—KISS!!!!"

"@therealsourdoughguy is going to be LIVID"

"please I'm begging for a why choose with @therealsourdoughguy and Chef Judas"

Gia snorts, reading out a few with her eyes gleaming. "Well, Charlie. The people want to know—are you single?"

I glance at her, then the camera, then back again. "Is this a live stream or a dating show?"

"That didn't sound like a no," she says sweetly.

"I plead the fifth."

She grins at the phone. "Translation: situationship confirmed."

I try to laugh it off, but something in my chest tightens. I want to say something—something that isn't a joke. But then—

Sniff.

Wait.

Shit.

Something smells... wrong.

I open the oven door, and my stomach sinks. The sponge is burnt around the edges, the smell unmistakable.

"Shit," I mutter, yanking it out with a tea towel. "Okay, we might've... slightly overshot golden brown."

Gia's already reaching for the phone to show the disaster to her followers, and I groan. "Please don't—"

She zooms in dramatically. "He tried his best, your honour."

My mind is racing, trying to figure out how to salvage this. I'm the one who's supposed to know what I'm doing, and I've just burned a basic sponge. On live video.

Fucking brilliant.

But then Gia laughs, and it's not mocking—it's warm. Lighthearted. Fucking adorable. "Hey, it's fine. That's what makes it fun, right? People love seeing the real stuff, even when it goes wrong."

Her words sink in, and I exhale, a small smile creeping onto my face. She's right. Maybe perfection isn't the point. I glance at the comments—some teasing, some supportive—and my nerves ease a little more;

"Watching Charlie panic-bake is better than any romcom I've ever seen."

"GIA HELP HIM :'(he looks like a sad golden retriever"

"We are ALL third-wheeling this livestream."

"He could burn my kitchen down and I'd thank him."

"Alright," I say, turning back to the camera. "Looks like we've got a bit of a fail here, but that's okay. We'll call it a test run. I'll whip up a new batch while Gia distracts you with her charm."

The smell of burnt sponge still lingers in the air, sharp and sour, as I scrape the charred mess into the bin. Across the kitchen, Gia is in her element—effortlessly holding the livestream together. Cool. Composed. Captivating. She's laughing, teasing the commenters, brushing off the disaster like it's part of the plan. She makes it look easy.

I grab the mixing bowl and start over. My hands move on instinct, but my head's somewhere else. This isn't just a second batch. It feels like something else entirely. A do-over. A shot at making something right—not just with the cake, but with her. With us.

I left. I ghosted my entire life when I flew to Australia. And she's made it clear she hasn't forgotten that.

Now, we're here again. Side by side. Familiar, but different. And I can't fuck it up.

She glances over just then, like she can feel the shift. "Want me to grab the orange zest?" she asks, already stepping closer.

"Yeah," I say, voice catching in my throat. "Thanks."

Our fingers touch for half a second when she passes the microplane. It shouldn't mean anything. But it does. It does, and I feel it everywhere.

I pour the egg replacement, fold in the flour, determined to get it right this time. I can feel the weight of Gia's presence beside me, the pull of all the unspoken things between us. It's not just about impressing her followers. Hell, it's not about them at all. It's about her. I don't want to let her down again.

I slide the new sponge into the oven, my heart pounding, but this time for different reasons. As I turn to face the camera, Gia flashes me a small smile, and it's like a lifeline.

"Take two," I say with a crooked grin, trying to ease the tension. "Let's hope this one doesn't end up as toast."

The comments roll in fast:

"The rolled-up sleeves are criminal. Arrest him."

"if Gia doesn't want him I'll take him. respectfully. or not."

"The hand veins. The Henley. I am unwell."

Gia reads them aloud, her laughter filling the room. "Looks like my followers have a crush on you," she teases, nudging me playfully.

I chuckle, shaking my head, but my nerves are still jangling inside. Gia wraps things up, cutting the live feed after promising her fans the full reel once the new batch has cooled and is ready to assemble.

As the screen fades to black, I glance at her, suddenly feeling the need to ask—no, to keep her here just a little longer. The idea hits me, half-formed but ready to go. I run with it before I can think too much.

"Y'know," I start, wiping my hands on a dish towel, "people seem pretty into this. Us. Working together." I shrug, pretending I'm nonchalant, though my pulse is hammering in my ears. "Maybe they'd want to see more of it. I could take you foraging sometime, show you a bit of what I do when I'm not burning cakes on live video."

Gia raises an eyebrow, her lips twitching like she's trying to figure out if I'm serious. "You mean. like, another live? Just... out in the wild?"

"Yeah, something like that," I say, though it's all a cover. I don't really care about the livestream, or her followers, or any of that. What I care about is more time with her. I'm disguising it as what they want, but the truth is, I just want to be near her. I don't know how long I'll have this chance, and I'm not about to waste it.

"Think they'd be into it," I add, trying to keep my tone casual. "Your followers seem to be, uh, thirsting for more."

Did I just say that? What a fucking loser.

Gia smirks, clearly clocking my thinly veiled excuse, but she doesn't call me out. Instead, she leans against the counter, arms folded. "Yeah? And what about you, Judas? You thirsting for more?"

9

CHARLIE

A Boy Brushed Red, Living in Black and White

My breath catches. She says it like a joke, but there's heat in her eyes—challenge, curiosity, something I shouldn't want as badly as I do. Am I thirsting for more? Fuck, yeah. But not just for the flirting or the attention. I want the version of us we never got to finish. The one we never even started.

Suddenly, it's just us. The noise from the comments, the buzz of performing, all of it fades, leaving a quiet, almost loaded silence. My heart's still beating too fast, the adrenaline of the live mixing with something else, something harder to ignore now that we're off-camera.

Gia's gaze is softer, but still sharp, like she's trying to figure me out all over again.

I clear my throat, trying to break the tension. "Well… that was a thing." My voice comes out too casual, like I'm trying to brush off the weight in the room. "Could've gone worse, right?"

She laughs, the sound easy, but there's an undercurrent I can't quite read. "You didn't set the kitchen on fire, so I'd call it a win."

I chuckle, pushing off the counter and moving toward her, my hands stuffed in my pockets. "Thanks for covering my ass out there." I gesture toward the phone. "You're kind of an enigma on camera. It's impressive."

She shrugs, leaning against the counter now, our bodies closer than before, though she doesn't seem to notice—or maybe she does, and she's just better at hiding it. "Guess I've had practice. But you're good too, Charlie. I mean, people were fangirling over you in the comments, so that's something, right?" She gives me a teasing smile, but there's heat in her eyes, even as she tries to downplay it.

I try to laugh it off, but the way she's looking at me, the way the air feels thicker now, makes it harder to stay relaxed. I'm painfully aware of how close we are, her perfume—sweet and sensual. Warm. Like summer wrapped itself around her and called her home. I catch her gaze and hold it for a beat longer than necessary.

"It's not about them, though," I murmur before I can stop myself.

She blinks, her eyebrows raising slightly. "No?"

"No," I admit, taking a step closer, barely a foot between us now. "It's about you."

Her lips part slightly, and for a second, I think maybe I've said too much. Maybe I've crossed a line we're both too afraid to acknowledge. But then she takes a breath, like she's steadying herself, and her gaze drops to my mouth before flicking back up to my eyes.

"And why's that, Charlie?" she asks, her voice low, the teasing edge gone now, replaced with something quieter, something real.

I swallow hard, feeling the weight of the years between us, of all the things left unsaid. I should step back. I should say something light, change the subject, keep this safe. But I don't. Instead, I take that final step, closing the gap until we're almost touching.

"Because I didn't want to screw this up," I say, my voice barely above a whisper. "Not again."

Her breath hitches, and for a second, the only sound in the room is the low hum of the oven and the faint ticking of the clock on the wall. She doesn't move, doesn't pull away, and I swear I can feel the pull between us, electric and undeniable.

I reach up, my fingers brushing a strand of hair behind her ear. Her skin is warm. Soft. And even though it's a small gesture, it sends a jolt through me. Gia's eyes flutter closed for the briefest moment, and when they open again, they're filled with something I haven't seen in a long time—something I've missed, even if I didn't realise it.

"I never stopped thinking about you," I confess, my thumb grazing her cheek. "Not once."

She's quiet for a beat, her breathing shallow. For a moment, it feels like the world stops spinning—just us in this quiet kitchen, surrounded by the soft sounds of our breath and the thudding of my heart.

"We can't do this," she whispers, but there's no conviction in her words.

Her hands rest on my chest, a light, uncertain touch. I don't know if she's pulling me closer or pushing me away. "Why not?"

"Because…" Her voice wavers, her fingers pressing against me, unsure if she's holding on or bracing herself to push away. "Because we shouldn't."

I swallow hard, caught between hope and restraint. "Tell me you don't want this, and I'll stop."

She hesitates, her lips parting as her chest rises and falls in shallow breaths. But the words never come.

Her silence lingers between us, thick and tense. But then Gia pulls back, stepping away from me, her hands dropping from my chest like I've burned her.

"No," she says, her voice sharp, her expression hard. "You don't get to do that."

I blink, stunned. "Do what?"

"This, Charlie." She gestures between us, her eyes blazing. "You don't get to act like you're some victim of time and circumstance. You did this."

"I missed you, Gia," I say softly, my chest tightening with the words. It feels like the most honest thing I've said in years.

Her laugh is cold, bitter, and it slices through me. "You don't get to say that when this is all your fault."

"Fault? What are you talking about?"

Just minutes ago, her hands were on my chest, her breath mingling with mine. Now, it's like there's a wall between us. No, not a wall—an ocean. Wide, cold, and filled with everything I never said.

"You're the one who left, Charlie. Not me. You!" Her voice rises, trembling with barely-contained frustration. "You walked away. You went to Australia. You left me here, alone, after everything."

"I didn't have a choice—"

"No, Charlie, you had a choice, and you chose to leave!" Her eyes are glassy, her anger turning raw, vulnerable. "Don't stand here and tell me you missed me when you're the one who disappeared. You don't get to act like you care, not after all these years. You weren't here."

I feel the weight of her words hit hard, like a punch I wasn't ready for. I drag a hand down my face, trying to swallow the guilt curdling in my gut. I want to fix this. I just don't know how. "I'm here now," I say, trying to keep my voice steady, but it's not enough.

She shakes her head, her arms crossing tightly over her chest like she's trying to hold herself together. "You can't just come back and act like everything's fine because it's not. It hasn't been fine for a long time."

"I know I messed up—"

"Messed up?" She cuts me off, her voice thick with disbelief. "You didn't just mess up, Charlie. You left. You were gone. For twelve years. And I had to deal with all of it—Nico's death, the aftermath, everything—on my own. And now you want to play the hero?"

I open my mouth to speak, but the words stick in my throat. She's right. I did leave. I ran when she needed me the most.

Gia takes a step back, her jaw clenched, her eyes never leaving mine. "You don't get to make it right just because you're back now."

The air between us feels too thick, like it's pressing in on me, suffocating. I take a breath, trying to find something to say that could make this better, but I come up empty. "Gia, I'm sorry."

"Sorry's not good enough," she snaps, her voice cracking just enough to make my heart ache. "Sorry doesn't change the fact that you left."

She turns away from me, her hands running through her hair in frustration. She doesn't cry. Not really. But her chin trembles, just once. She blinks hard, like she's trying to erase the shimmer in her eyes. And when she crosses her arms again, it's not defiance, it's armour.

For the first time since I've been back, I see just how deeply I hurt her. It's not just anger. It's grief. Disappointment. Everything I caused by walking away.

"I'm not expecting things to be the same," I say quietly. "But I came back to make things right."

She laughs again, but it's hollow. "You can't fix this, Charlie. You can't just show up and think it'll all go away."

"I'm trying," I say, my voice rising slightly, my own frustration slipping through.

"Well, try harder," she snaps, her eyes blazing as she meets my gaze again. "Because right now, all I see is the guy who abandoned me."

I flinch as if she's slapped me, the words slicing clean through my chest. Her eyes gleam, not just with fury, but with hurt so sharp it takes the air out of my lungs.

She shakes her head, stepping back until her spine hits the edge of the counter. Her fingers dig into it like she needs the grounding, like she might fall apart if she doesn't hold onto something.

"I can't do this," Gia says, her voice tight, like she's trying to hold back more than just the words.

My heart drops. The anger in her eyes has cooled to something worse—defeat. Like she's already made up her mind that we're a lost cause.

"Gia..." I take a step toward her, but she turns away.

"No, Charlie." Her voice is shaking. Her hands, too. "You don't get to waltz back in and expect me to just... what? Pretend like everything's fine? Like you didn't leave me here to deal with everything while you got to escape?"

I stand there, dumbfounded, feeling like the biggest asshole in the world. "I didn't mean to—"

"You never mean to." She cuts me off, her voice sharp but cracking at the edges. "You didn't mean to leave, you didn't mean to disappear, but you still did. And I was here. I was the one who had to stay and watch my family fall apart."

I open my mouth to say something, anything to make it better, but nothing comes. What could I say that she hasn't already heard?

"You don't understand," she whispers. "You just... don't." Her eyes hold a quiet hurt that presses down on me, heavier than any words could.

"I never asked you to wait for me." I regret my words the moment they leave my mouth.

She lets out a bitter laugh. "No, you didn't. You didn't ask me for anything, Charlie. You just left. You didn't even give me a choice."

Her words hit me like a hammer, knocking the wind out of me. I watch her, standing there in my kitchen, the same place we just laughed together in front of the camera, and now she's unravelling. But the truth is—she's right. I left. I made that decision.

I reach for her, desperate to pull her back, but she's already retreating. Her eyes are bright with unshed tears, her voice thick with the pain I caused.

"I'm sorry," I repeat with more conviction, though I know it's not enough. It's not even close. "I thought I was doing the right thing. After Nico—"

"Don't," she cuts in, voice sharp, almost breaking. "Don't use my brother as an excuse for why you ran."

I flinch. That's exactly what I've been doing, isn't it? I ran to escape the guilt, the grief that came with Nico's death. I thought leaving would make it easier for her, for both of us. But now, standing in front of her, seeing the anger and hurt etched into every line of her face, I realise how wrong I was.

"You didn't even—" She cuts herself off, her voice cracking with emotion, and I feel my heart shatter a little more.

"Gia..." I take a step closer, the distance between us unbearable, and I see the conflict in her eyes. "Please. Let me try to fix this. Let me fix us."

She shakes her head, a tear slipping down her cheek before she steels herself. And I know that I'm losing her. "How can you fix something that's been broken for so long?"

For a moment, I don't know what to say. How do I convince her that I'm not the same man who left? That I want to stay now? That I won't make the same mistake twice?

"I don't know," I admit, my voice low. "But I'll do whatever it takes. I'll try, Gia. Just... don't walk away."

I feel like I'm on the edge of a cliff, the ground crumbling beneath me.

"This was a mistake," she says, her voice steady. "I shouldn't have come here. I shouldn't have agreed to this."

With every step she takes toward the door, I feel the space between us grow, the distance I've tried to bridge now feeling insurmountable.

"Gia... please." My voice is thick, barely a whisper, and it stops her in her tracks. But she doesn't turn around, no matter how much I will her to.

"No," she finally says. "Not now. Not like this."

She pushes the door open, and I watch her go, the door swinging shut behind her with a finality that feels like a punch to the gut.

I don't move. I let her go. Because maybe she's right. Maybe showing up doesn't mean I deserve a second chance.

The door closes behind her, and the kitchen falls into silence again. Same four walls. Same ticking clock. But everything feels different now.

I lean against the counter, staring at the half-finished ingredients scattered around. This was supposed to be a fresh start, a chance to reconnect, but instead, I've just reopened old wounds.

I don't know how to fix this, how to make her see that I've changed, that I want to be better—not just for myself, but for her. But with her gone, I'm left with the echo of her words ringing in my ears, the truth of my past choices crashing down like a tidal wave.

"Fuck," I mutter to myself, frustration boiling over just as the smell of smoke fills the kitchen.

Fuck. Fuck. *Fuck.*

I can't lose her again. I won't.

10

GIA

For You, and Your Denial

I hate how I still feel him. How every inch, every nerve, remembers. How my body—the traitorous little bitch—still wants him.

Fucking Charlie.

I can't let him break me again. I *won't*.

Still, my mind clings to every word he said, replaying them in a loop I can't shut off. No matter how loud I blast the music, it doesn't drown out his voice.

"I'm sorry."

Fuck his apology.

I crank the volume higher, the bass rattling through the car, and step on the gas. My heart's racing, my thoughts scattered. I just need to get home. Away from him. Away from everything.

My grip tightens on the wheel as pressure builds in my chest. The road's just movement and noise. My thoughts are stuck on him—his hands, those ocean-fucking-eyes, the taste of what almost was.

A blur of motion flashes to my right. My heart lurches.

A cyclist.

I slam the brake just as they swerve, narrowly missing my front bumper.

Shit.

I'm shaking. My pulse pounds in my ears as the panic rushes in. For a moment, I can't breathe. My hands grip the steering wheel so tightly my knuckles are white.

They flip me off, shouting something I can't make out, before riding off. They must've been a teen—too young to know how close that was. How close I came to—

I pull off to the side of the road, body trembling, and it all hits me at once. The panic, the grief, the anger. A scream tears from my throat before I even realise it, raw and jagged and aching, breaking the silence of the empty street.

I can't go home. I don't want to sit in that silent house with my racing thoughts and a glass of wine that won't fix anything.

So instead, I turn the car around.

By the time I reach the cemetery, the sky's bruised with the first blush of dusk. The air is cool, the kind of quiet that feels sacred. I make my way across the gravel path, my boots crunching softly beneath me until I reach Nico's headstone.

My throat tightens.

"Hey," I whisper, sinking down into the grass beside him. "It's been a while."

Like I don't say that every time I come here.

I brush a few stray leaves away from the stone, fingers trembling. "I almost hit someone today. A kid. Just a blur and I nearly... it was too close."

My hand drifts to a blade of grass, twisting it between my fingers.

"Charlie's back. But you already know that." The words fall flat in the quiet. "I thought I was okay. Thought I had it together." I let out a bitter laugh. "Then he apologised. He said he was sorry, Nico, and everything inside me just... fell apart."

I draw in a shaky breath and rest my hand against the stone.

"You remember that night? I do. Every fucking second of it."

I close my eyes, and the memory drags me under like a rip current.

A party. A phone call. A siren. Flashing lights racing past the house—the ones I mistook for strobes.

"I still wonder if things would've been different if you'd just said yes. If you'd gotten on the damn bike with Charlie, instead of your own. Maybe I'd have lost you both. Maybe neither of you."

I pause, swallowing hard.

"But you were trying to do the right thing. You always were."

My voice breaks. The truth presses heavy on my chest, and I let the tears fall freely now.

"I hate that he's back. I hate that he made it out and you didn't. And I hate that part of me still wants to know if he's okay."

My phone buzzes in my pocket.

I almost ignore it. But I don't.

> *Charlie: Hey. I know today didn't go as planned, but I didn't want it to be a complete waste.*

Then a second message. Then photos.

He's remade the jelly ear jaffa cakes.

The lighting's off. The shots are wobbly. But they're honest. Trying. Soft around the edges in a way that almost hurts. Charlie's never been afraid to feel. To cry. To care—even when it made things harder. His softness was always one of the reasons I loved him.

> *Charlie: I'm not a pro or anything, but I thought maybe you could use them. Sorry they're not up to your usual standard, but… maybe they'll help?*

My chest tightens.

Of course he's trying to fix things. That's always been his way. Patch it together. Make it *less bad.* Even now, after everything.

And I don't know whether to cry harder or throw my phone into the nearest headstone.

11

GIA

The Quiet Things That No One Ever Knows

"C'mon, G, it'll be fun," Olive says, her voice bouncing through the speaker.

I roll my eyes, slicing a tomato with more force than necessary. "Ols, you know I don't sing."

There's a pause, and I can hear her moving around on the other end, probably multitasking as usual.

"I know. But maybe it's time to break that silence. Just a little."

I don't answer right away.

"Oooorrr..." she says, with a teasing edge. "I'll do the singing, and you can just watch me make a tit out of myself. I thrifted this sick Gerard Way jacket, and it's screaming for an emo karaoke night."

I bite back a smile but keep chopping. A cucumber rolls off the board. I don't bother picking it up.

"So you only want me to go out with you so you can cosplay?"

"I think you could use a night out," Olive says, her voice softening in that way that makes me feel like I'm being coddled.

I shake my head, dumping the chopped veggies into the bowl. "And emo karaoke is supposed to fix all my problems?" I say, sarcasm dripping from every word.

"Maybe not all of them, but..." She lets the sentence dangle, and I stare down at the salad, my grip tightening on the knife. The kitchen suddenly feels too quiet, even with Olive's voice filling the space.

I sigh, reach for the fridge, and grab the dressing. "Look, I'm fine. I don't need a night out."

"Fine? G, when's the last time you did something fun? Or, like, something that wasn't work or food-related?" Olive asks, her tone shifting from playful to serious.

I pause mid-pour, watching the dressing glop out. The sound is louder than it should be. "I have fun."

"You have controlled, structured fun where you can't let loose for even a second," she counters. "Karaoke, costumes, a few drinks—it'll be good for you."

I shake my head, though she can't see it. "I'm not getting up on stage in front of a crowd."

Olive groans. "You don't have to! We can hang out, people-watch, sing along from our seats. Besides, don't you miss the good old days? When you used to hit up concerts and scream the lyrics like your life depended on it?"

I hesitate. The blade clinks against the counter as I set the knife down. Images flash through my mind—the tangle of sweaty bodies in a mosh pit, black eyeliner, busted Converse. The kind of screaming that felt like freedom. I haven't let myself think about that in years.

"Those days are long gone, Ols," I mutter. tossing the salad half-heartedly. Lettuce flops out over the rim of the bowl. I don't bother scooping it back in.

"They don't have to be." Her voice is soft now, a quiet nudge. "Just one night, Gia. You might surprise yourself."

I don't respond right away, my hand resting on the edge of the counter, salad forgotten. Olive doesn't get it—she never knew Nico, never felt that kind of loss, the kind that settles in your bones and turns everything grayscale. But that's part of why I've kept her close. She reminds me of the girl I used to be, before the grief hollowed her out.

"Gia," Olive says, more serious now. "You've been going through the motions for years. Don't you want to feel alive again? Even just for a night?"

I roll my eyes, mostly out of habit. "And karaoke is your solution to that?"

"It's not just karaoke. It's a night to stop thinking, to stop planning, and just be."

I lean back against the counter, letting the cool surface press into my spine. Olive is relentless, but she's not wrong. I can't remember the last time I did something that wasn't measured, safe, expected.

"I don't know," I say, but my voice lacks conviction.

"You don't have to know," she presses. "You just have to show up. I'll handle the rest. You and me, a couple of drinks, some terrible singing, and maybe a ridiculous costume or two. Come on, what's the worst that could happen?"

I smirk despite myself. "I could die of secondhand embarrassment."

"Oh, please. If you've survived me this long, you'll survive this."

I laugh. And for a second, the weight on my chest lifts. I can almost see it—Olive on stage, belting out early 2000s angst while I sip something strong and pretend I don't know her. Bad singing, worse outfits, and the two of us letting go—something I haven't allowed myself to do in far too long.

"I'll think about it," I say, and this time, I mean it.

"Good enough for now," she chirps. "But I'm not letting this go, G. I'll make sure you have no choice but to say yes."

We hang up. I rinse the salad dressing off my fingers, but I don't go back to chopping.

Instead, I open Spotify. My finger hovers over a playlist I haven't touched in years: *Stolen Tracks*—the one with all the songs I used to sneak from Nico's room. He never minded. God, I miss the sound of CDs clicking into place, the way music used to feel like something real.

I don't press play.

But I look. I memorise. I remember.

And for now, it's enough.

12

GIA

This Ain't A Scene, It's an Arms Race

The bar is dimly lit, thick with laughter, off-key singing, and the unmistakable funk of beer and sweat. Emo karaoke night is in full swing—a sea of black band tees, plaid skirts, and more studded belts than I've seen in a decade.

I tug at the hem of my skirt, a cool draft sneaking through the holes in my fishnets.

I'm far too old for this shit.

"I can't believe you talked me into this," I mutter, shooting a sideways glance at Olive, who's practically buzzing with smug satisfaction.

She grins, the silver stripes on her Black Parade knockoff jacket catching the neon bar lights like a disco ball. "Oh, come on, G! We're just reliving our glory days—like Gen X at eighties night."

I snort. "Yeah, except for the fact that I haven't dressed like this in... what? Ten years?" I glance down at my half-hearted cosplay of Vic Fuentes; white dress shirt, black tie, black mini skirt, fishnets, and a pair of chucks. Olive had practically thrown the fishnets at me when we were getting ready, and now here I am—full emo revival mode.

"You look hot," Olive says with zero hesitation. "Trust me, no one cares that you haven't rocked fishnets since college. You blend."

I scan the room again. She's not wrong—everyone here looks like they've stepped out of an emo time capsule. And while part of me feels like I'm faking it, another part is kind of looking forward to it. The music, the vibe—it's dredging up memories of late nights at dingy concert venues and that reckless, carefree feeling I haven't let myself indulge in for years.

"You're still not getting me up on stage," I say, arms folded across my chest.

Olive rolls her eyes. "You don't have to sing. I'm just glad you're here."

I spot someone dressed head to toe like Pete Wentz—eyeliner smudged in all the right places, black skinny jeans tight enough to cut off circulation. A few feet away, there's a guy fully committed to his Brendon Urie era—top hat and all.

"Look at everyone else—they're having a blast. The drinks are cheap, the music's perfect, and we're basically in a room full of our people." She nods toward the stage, where someone is currently massacring a Panic! At The

Disco song. "You've already made it this far. Just relax, have fun, and who knows? You might surprise yourself."

I arch a brow. "This is me having fun, Ols."

She narrows her eyes at me, unconvinced. "Oh, please. You're still thinking about work. Or recipes. Or something equally boring like rearranging your spice rack."

"I am not!" I protest, even though... yeah, she's probably right. Some part of my brain is still stuck on the meal prep I didn't finish earlier and the vlog I need to edit before Monday.

Still, something about the room—about the nostalgia laced in the music and the too-loud speakers—is starting to loosen something in me. Just a little.

We order our drinks, and I find us a table while Olive signs her life away to the karaoke gods. My foot taps along to the rhythm, and my fingers twitch with the urge to drum out the beat on the tabletop—muscle memory from a past life I almost forgot was mine.

God, I really am an elder emo.

"Admit it," Olive says when she returns, leaning in with a glint in her eye. "You're enjoying this more than you thought."

I bite back a smile. "Maybe a little."

She grins wider. "Good. Now, what'll it take to get you to loosen up even more? Vodka? Tequila?"

I shake my head. "No shots," I say, but my voice is already softer. The nostalgia is hitting hard now, and though I won't admit it out loud, Olive's right—it feels kind of good to be here. It feels like home.

"I'm still not singing," I add, just to be clear

"Yet," she says with a wink, draining the rest of her drink. "I'll wear you down. Just wait."

"That's what you think."

She hops up, practically vibrating with energy. "Alright, I'm getting more drinks. Don't move."

Shots for one, I guess.

I pull out my phone, ready to catch a few candid moments. The scene is a mess—off-key vocals, wild gestures, enough hair product to ignite a small fire. The group on stage is attempting to harmonise to All Time Low, and failing miserably. But it's kind of perfect.

And then—my heart does a little flip.

Charlie's here.

Tight white t-shirt. Black skinny jeans. Classic black Converse. A black motorcycle helmet tucked under one arm like he's straight out of a YA daydream. His hair falls messily across his forehead, serving full emo boy vibes. He looks effortlessly cool, in that maddening kind of way that makes my stomach flutter and my heart trip over itself.

He scans the room. I see his eyes land on Olive first, then me. My stomach twists as a wave of something crashes over me. Nostalgia, maybe. Regret. Hope.

He smiles. Small. Soft. One of those half-smiles that hits like a sucker punch to the ribs.

Then he turns away.

Warmth floods my chest, but it's tangled with guilt. Guilt for how I tore into him the last time we spoke. Sometimes I forget he lost his best friend that day too.

I'm not sure what I feel, exactly. Happy? Off-balance? Blindsided, for sure. Part of me wonders if Olive planned this. It's exactly her kind of meddling.

"Would you look at that," she says, right on cue. "Charlie's here."

"You invited him?" I ask, my voice already doing that pitchy thing it does when I'm trying to pretend I'm cool.

She shrugs. "Maybe I did. Maybe I didn't. You'll never prove it."

I stare at her, somewhere between annoyed and lowkey grateful.

"He keeps looking this way," I mutter.

"Then go say hi."

I freeze. My brain stutters. "I wouldn't even know what to say."

Olive rolls her eyes. "Like that's ever stopped you."

I groan. "This is so embarrassing."

"Embrace the cringe, Gia. You've got this."

I don't, but okay.

Just as I'm considering whether or not to make a break for the bathroom, he walks over.

"Hey, Charlie," Olive chirps, way too pleased with herself.

"Olive. Good to see you." Then he turns to me. "Gia. Hey."

"Hey," I say, suddenly aware of my entire body. My posture. My breathing. My hair. Why didn't I wear something hotter?

"You here to rescue me from karaoke?" he asks, a crooked grin playing at his mouth. "You're the best singer I know, after all."

Olive laughs, her voice light. "Oh, that's hilarious. Gia doesn't sing."

"Sure she does," Charlie replies, looking genuinely confused. "Voice of a fucking angel."

I roll my eyes, heat rising to my cheeks. "No. Olive's right. I don't sing," I clip.

Charlie blinks. "Since when?"

"Since always," I say firmly, the words coming out sharper than I meant.

Charlie raises an eyebrow, a hint of a smile tugging at his lips. "But karaoke is supposed to be fun. You can't just sit there and watch us."

I fold my arms, fingers digging into my sleeves. "That's exactly what I'll do. Sit here, sip my drink, and judge everyone mercilessly."

Olive chimes in, "But everyone sings at karaoke. It's the law."

"Okay, seriously, can we drop this?" I snap. "I'm not singing. End of."

Instant regret.

Charlie raises his hands in mock surrender. "Alright, alright. No pressure."

But the air shifts. Just slightly.

Olive doesn't say anything at first. Just watches me with that look—part concern, part quiet patience.

And I hate that I snapped at her. Hate the sharp edge in my voice. But I don't want to explain. I don't want to unwrap the memories tied like chains around my vocal cords.

She finally speaks, her voice low. "I get it. I've got you, okay?"

I exhale, tension leaking from my shoulders. "I know. I'm sorry."

She squeezes my hand. I force a smile.

I really don't deserve her.

Charlie glances between us—curious, cautious. Like he's weighing whether to say something. Then he just nods, like he gets it. And maybe that's what I appreciate most.

We sit. The music plays on. And for now, I just let myself be in it. Awkward silence and all.

13

CHARLIE

...Slowdance on the Inside

I don't know what sucks more—watching Gia shut down like that, or knowing I'm part of the reason why. I wanted tonight to be light, fun, a reset. But she's wound so tight it's like she's bracing for impact. And all I want is to take it away. The heaviness, the grief. I want to make her forget, even just for one song.

My name gets called. I'm heading for the stage before I have the chance to back out. Then the first notes of "A Little Less Sixteen Candles" echo through the bar.

As I start to sing, I scan the crowd—careful not to zero in on her too hard. I don't want to make it obvious, don't want this to feel like a plea, even if that's exactly what it is. I tell myself it's just a performance. That I'm just having fun.

But every time the lyrics hit a little too close to home, I find her eyes. I make sure she sees me. Feels it.

This song might as well have been written about me—fucking up, missing my shot. And by the look on her face, she knows it too.

I dive into the chorus, pouring everything I have into the words as the audience repeats them right back to me. It's more than nostalgia. It's us. It's the moments we lost, the ones I'd give anything to rewrite.

As I finish the last note, the applause washes over me, and I catch a glimpse of Gia again. Her eyes are brighter. Her smirk says *nice try*, but there's something genuine underneath.

"Not bad," she says, tilting her head.

"Just warming up." I lean in. "Wait till you see what I've got up my sleeve next."

"Wait, you mean we get more of this?" she says, gesturing to my whole self with a teasing grin.

"Only if you're lucky," I reply, keeping my tone light.

"God, you're so cheesy." She shakes her head with a laugh.

"Cheesy? I thought I was charming," I counter, not missing a beat.

"Charming, huh? We'll see about that," she replies, her eyes sparkling with playful challenge.

I'm ready with another comeback, already halfway into the grin that goes with it—

"Ugh, get a room," Olive groans, cutting in with perfect timing. But she's smirking, already standing.

Before I can shoot back, her name's called.

"Get ready for a classic!" she announces, practically skipping to the stage as the crowd roars.

The opening chords of "Misery Business" hit, and the bar erupts.

Olive's thriving. Gia… not so much.

She's gone still. That thousand-yard stare. Like she's somewhere else entirely.

And I know where.

Nico's funeral.

She hasn't sung since. I see it now—the tightness in her jaw, the way her fingers twitch like they want to move but can't. She's not just remembering. She's *reliving* it.

I lean close. "Hey. You wanna get out of here?"

She startles. Eyes wide for a beat. Then she exhales, softer now. "What did you have in mind?"

"I don't know. Have you eaten?" I ask, hoping it'll be enough to pull her out of whatever she's stuck in.

Gia glances around the bar, then shrugs—shoulders loosening, like maybe, finally, she's ready to let go of the weight she's been dragging all night. "I can always eat, Chef."

Chef.

The way she says it—light, teasing, like it means nothing—sends blood straight to my dick.

Relief punches through me. A crack in the wall.

"Then let's go," I say, already half-standing.

"We can't just leave," she says, nodding toward Olive.

The rejection stings sharper than I expect. This wasn't some grand seduction plan—just a chance to reset. A win would be getting her to like me again, maybe even laugh. But whatever shifted between us a second ago? It's slipping, and I don't know how to hold it in place.

I stay quiet, even though everything in me wants to reach for her.

But then she turns back to me, eyes scanning my face like she's searching for something she doesn't quite trust is there. Her voice drops. "Why are you looking at me like that?"

I swallow. "I don't know. Thought maybe you needed a breather."

Her smile falters, just a flicker, but enough to make my chest tighten. "You're not wrong," she says softly.

Still, she hesitates. And for a second, I think I've misread it all. That maybe I should back off.

Then Olive barrels over, breathless and glowing. "That was a rush."

"You killed it," I say, and she lights up.

Gia watches her, but I can see it—the way she starts folding inward again. That slow retreat back behind her walls.

I try one last push. "I almost wish I hadn't signed up for another song."

She lifts a brow. "Nobody's holding a gun to your head."

"I know. I just wanted you to hear it."

That gets her. She looks at me—really looks at me. A pause. A breath. Something sharp and electric pulling taut between us.

"You know what? Fuck it. Let's go," she says.

"What, you're ditching me?" Olive calls out, loud enough to draw a few looks. She clutches her chest in mock betrayal, but the mischievous glint in her eye gives her away. "I'm just messing—honestly, you two are so bloody boring anyway. Besides, there's a guy over there with spider bites who spent that entire song eye-fucking me."

"Ugh, TMI, Ols," Gia groans, but there's a glint in her eye too now—softer, lighter.

Olive grins and pulls her into a hug, murmuring something in Gia's ear that I can't quite catch. Gia nods, lips twitching like she's fighting a smile.

Then Olive turns to me, already backing away. "Don't do anything I wouldn't do."

"Will she be alright?" I ask, watching as Olive saunters toward a group of guys in band tees and enough facial piercings to set off airport security.

Gia snorts, shooting me a side-eye. "Olive? Please. She's been doing mixed martial arts since she was four. She could dropkick you in platforms and not spill her drink."

I raise my hands in surrender. "Noted."

Fuck, I'm nervous. Not about the ass-kicking—Olive could absolutely take me down in Doc Martens and a glitter crop top—but she's been nothing but a gem to me tonight. Inviting me out. Giving me a shot. If I didn't know any better, I'd say she's rooting for me and Gia.

And I wish I could pretend I don't know why. But my heart, my hands, my dick, and the bloody Pope all know exactly why: this five-foot-five spitfire beside me is the reason my nerves are shot and my body's running hot like a furnace.

Outside, the cool night air smacks into us. It should help. It doesn't.

She clocks my bike and raises a brow. "Still riding that death trap?"

Death trap.

The words knock the breath out of me. Nico's voice, clear as day, slams into my chest like a punch I didn't see coming.

"It's *a fucking death trap, mate.*" He said it with a grin that didn't quite reach his eyes. I should've known something was off.

I blink hard, forcing the memory back into its box before I choke on the past. "How else am I supposed to look hot getting around?" I say, aiming for cocky, but the smile feels off—stretched too thin.

I unclip the spare helmet and offer it to her—yeah, presumptuous, but I'm glad I grabbed it. Some part of me must've hoped we'd get here.

She rolls her eyes but takes it anyway. "Hot, or reckless? There's a fine line, you know."

"Hot and reckless is my brand," I say, securing my helmet before helping with hers.

She smirks. "I guess some things never change." As she adjusts the helmet, my fingers brush her neck—just light enough to make a shiver ripple through her.

I pretend not to notice, though I catch the quick hitch in her breath and the way her skin prickles under my touch. "Need a boost?" I ask, nodding toward the bike.

"Very funny." She hikes a leg up over the bike and slides onto the seat, then shuffles back to give me space.

"Cute how hard you're trying to hate me right now, G."

"Cute how I value your opinion." Her voice is low and a little teasing, but the grin tugging at her lips gives her away.

I swing my leg over the bike, the seat warm from where she's been sitting. Settling in front of her, I rev the engine.

"Now, hold on tight," I tease, glancing back. "Unless you think I'm fragile or something?"

"Please," she mutters, tightening her grip. "You're not fooling anyone."

The engine hums beneath us. Her body presses into mine, warm and real and *here*.

Let's see who's fooling who.

14

GIA

Bike Scene

I swing off the back of Charlie's bike, tugging off the helmet and shaking out my hair as I glance up at The Boathouse. "Twice in one week?" I say, eyeing the little wooden gate that leads to his place. "People might start talking."

I should know better than to flirt. But it slips out before I can stop it.

He smirks, kicking the stand down and tugging off his gloves. "What's up, Perelli? Scared to be alone with me?"

I arch a brow, lips curving into a smirk. There's a quiet charge in the air—the kind that fills the space between breaths. The street is still, and it amplifies the hum building between us.

Then my phone buzzes somewhere in my bag, slicing through the moment. I dig it out and glance at the screen.

Olive: Please tell me he's taking you down under?

She's impossible. Always on brand. Always slightly obsessed with my sex life—or the glaring lack of it.

I bite back a laugh and glance at Charlie, who's currently wrestling with the wooden gate.

Rolling my eyes, I fire off a reply.

Gia: Oh yeah, he's rocked my world. Don't know how I'll ever recover from his 12-inch boomerang. Totally ruined me for life

I tuck my phone away just as the gate flies open.

I head up the steps first, triggering the balcony light. The kitchen still holds the heat of the afternoon sun, that same rustic space I stood in days ago. The window's flung wide open, the ocean stretching out beyond it, breeze cutting through the salt-heavy air.

Charlie sets his helmet on the counter and heads for the fridge. "What'll it be? I've got... ramen?" He holds up a Tupperware tub of broth and noodles like it's a prize.

I squint at it. "You're joking."

"Nope."

"You're a literal chef, and you're offering me leftovers from a student flat share?"

He chuckles, setting it on the counter. "First of all, rude. Second—this is homemade broth. Kombu, shiitake, miso—the good stuff. Took me six hours."

I blink. "You spent six hours making fancy ramen and put it in a plastic tub?"

"Old habits die hard," he says with a grin. "When I first moved to Australia, I was broke as hell. Lived on instant ramen and boxed wine for months."

I cross my arms, leaning against the counter. "Sounds tragic."

"It was character-building."

I snort. "Your gut must've hated you."

"Barely," he says, grabbing a couple of bowls. "But hey, I got creative. Learned how to stretch scraps into something decent. I still crave it, even now."

There's a softness in his voice—nostalgia, maybe—but he masks it with a quick glance. "Anyway. You in or not?"

I nod, slow and deliberate. "Only if I get a real bowl."

"Deal. Just try not to wear it this time."

I smirk. "Who says I'm not into getting a little messy?"

His eyes flicker—something darker now, deeper. The air between us shifts, thickens. "Careful what you wish for, Perelli."

"Please, I'm just here for the food," I say, crossing my arms and leaning against the counter, trying to keep it breezy even as my heart stutters in my chest. "But it definitely helps that I'm in good company."

"Good company always makes the food taste better."

A soft silence settles between us, broken only by the distant hush of waves and the clink of spoons as he heats the broth on the stove.

Charlie hands me a bowl, steam curling into the air. I cradle it in both hands, take a tentative sip—and pause, surprised by the depth of flavour.

"Okay, that's actually amazing," I say, cradling the bowl like it's something sacred.

He smirks. "Told you. Sometimes the simplest stuff hits hardest."

I glance out the window, where the ocean glistens under the moonlight, silver and still. "It must be nice... waking up here."

"You know me... I always loved the beach."

"I know." I hesitate, fingers tightening slightly around the bowl. "Did you ever think about coming back?"

"All the time."

The kitchen quietens even more, the silence stretching between us like thread. I take a breath, the weight of everything we haven't said pressing down on my chest. "I thought about you a lot over the years, Charlie."

His hands still for a moment, then he looks at me—really looks. There's something raw in his eyes, a flicker of something vulnerable.

"Me too," he says quietly. "More than I probably should have."

I hesitate, then give voice to the thought that's been haunting me. "Sometimes I wonder if things would've been different... if Nico was still here."

Charlie's jaw tightens, the weight of my brother's name thickening the air between us. "He was the reason I stayed away for so long," he says, his voice rough. "But also why I couldn't stay away forever."

I nod slowly, the silence between us heavy with memory. "He meant a lot to both of us."

Charlie steps closer, close enough that I can feel the warmth radiating off him. "Yeah. And maybe that's why this—" he gestures between us, a slight lift of his hand, careful, reverent—"matters even more now."

The night feels different now—deeper, more grounded. Like we've stepped into something real. And for once, the distance we've kept between us slips away, leaving just this moment. Just us.

Charlie smirks, his voice low and warm. "You know, tonight made me think about the night we met. Remember?"

I nod, a small smile tugging at my lips. "How could I forget."

He's talking about the gig—the night Nico busted me when I was supposed to be studying for my exams.

But even as I say it, another memory flickers—one he doesn't know about.

The night of that party I sneaked into.

I spotted him across the crowded room. He was sitting on the couch, smoke curling from his lips, an easy, effortless smile lighting his face as he laughed at something someone said. I remember thinking he didn't look real—like he'd stepped straight out of some angsty dreamscape. Sharp jawline, worn band tee, one hand stuffed in his pocket, the other casually holding a cigarette—like that Alanis song. It was like he had nowhere to be, yet somehow was the reason people showed up.

And I just... watched.

But I don't say any of that. Not yet.

He leans back against the counter, eyes never leaving mine. "You've always been fierce, G. Never needed saving.

But it doesn't mean you can't let someone else take the reins for a while."

I still. "I know. I'm just... not used to it. Having someone care like that." I bite back a smile. "But you were pretty persistent."

"Still am," he says with a grin. "But that night... it stuck with me."

I give him a playful nudge. "I have that effect on people."

Charlie chuckles under his breath, rising to gather our empty bowls. He carries them to the sink and runs the tap, rinsing them one by one. It's quiet. Easy. Familiar in a way I didn't expect.

"I'm sorry I laid into you the other day. You didn't deserve that."

He pauses for a moment before replying. "It's okay."

It's not. His back is still turned, so I can't read his expression, but the conviction in his voice sounds genuine.

I shift my weight, trying to read the mood. Then he glances over his shoulder. "Hey... do you feel like staying for a crappy movie?"

I raise an eyebrow. "How crappy are we talking?"

"Like... low-budget shark attack meets bad CGI tornado levels of crap."

I snort. "Sounds perfect, actually."

The water shuts off. He turns, drying his hands on a tea towel. "You're welcome to stay if you want. No funny business. I just... it's late.

I hesitate, then say it before I can second-guess myself. "Would that be weird?"

His answer is immediate, soft. "Doesn't have to be."

We stand there, staring, silent and suspended in something I can't name.

My collar suddenly feels tighter, the waistband of my skirt digging into my stomach now that I'm no longer distracted by adrenaline or awkward tension. Then reality kicks in, and the weight of the evening settles back on my skin.

"Hey, do you have anything offensively baggy I can change into?" I tug at my tie with a groan. "This outfit's cute and all, but it's also kind of a prison."

Charlie chuckles, nodding toward the hallway. "Top drawer, bottom drawer—honestly, take your pick."

"Thanks," I say, and head off in the direction he pointed.

His bedroom is soft in a way I didn't expect—crisp white sheets, a couple of leafy plants thriving in mismatched pots, crystals lined neatly along the windowsill. A stack of dog-eared paperbacks sits on the nightstand. It's cosy, lived-in, calm.

It's Charlie.

I dig through the drawers and find a pair of gym shorts and an oversized T-shirt that smells like clean laundry... and something else. Something that's just him—warm, a little woodsy, the faintest trace of whatever scent he wears but never overdoes. I pull it over my head, the fabric swallowing me whole, and try not to like it as much as I do.

When I return, he looks up from the couch, eyes flicking over me with a lazy sort of smile. "Well, damn. You wear stolen clothes well."

I roll my eyes, padding barefoot across the room. "You offering tea or just compliments tonight?"

"Both," he says, already getting to his feet. "Chamomile or mint?"

"Dealer's choice."

By the time he returns with two mismatched mugs, I've curled into one corner of the couch, tucking my legs under me. He sinks into the opposite end, throwing a blanket over us like it's the most natural thing in the world. The movie's already started—terrible CGI sharks flying through what looks like a desert storm.

We sip in silence, the tension of the day unravelling with every ridiculous plot twist. I'm half-asleep by the time a shark crashes through a diner window on-screen.

"Jesus Christ," Charlie mutters. "This thing deserves an Oscar."

I let out a sleepy laugh, my head lolling toward him. The last thing I hear before sleep claims me is his voice—low and laced in warmth.

"Sleep tight, G."

15

CHARLIE

If I'm James Dean, You're Audrey Hepburn

The hot spray of the shower beats down on me as I try to wash away the buzz from the night. I'm wired, wide awake, with sleep nowhere near my radar. My thoughts keep drifting back to Gia—how she's asleep, on my couch. How she ended up here. How vulnerable she was when she apologised, as if I needed it. I only ever needed her to be okay.

There was a sadness in her eyes last night, something deep and familiar. I can handle her anger—that fire, that spark—but the sadness? That's what wrecks me. Watching it dim her, watching it steal the light from her... it's like being eighteen again and realising too late that sometimes love can't save someone from their own grief.

I won't lie—I spent most of the night watching her sleep like some obsessed stalker. Over the years, I tried to hold on to the details—how her laugh creases the skin by her eyes, the way she taps her fingers when she's thinking, how she chews her lip when she's holding something in. But memory blurs things. I tried to sketch her from scraps, and somewhere along the line, I started getting the lines wrong.

But now? She's right there.

Even now, I can see her—curled on the couch, blanket kicked off, one leg hiked up like she owns the damn space. My shirt slipping off her shoulder. Stirring in her sleep, lips parting around words I can't make out. And I wonder... maybe she gets up. Maybe she walks barefoot down the hall, rubbing at her eyes. Maybe she pauses just outside the bathroom door, just close enough that I can feel her.

"Gia," I breathe, her name slipping out like a prayer.

Daydream or not, I'm staying.

Warm hands trace around me, circling to my stomach. Her touch is soft—tentative, reverent. She explores slowly, like she's savouring every second.

I dip my head, eyes closing. The warmth of her palms against my skin sends sparks straight through me. Every brush of her fingertips pulls me under, fogging my brain, flooding my chest.

I've imagined this a hundred times.

What if I fuck it up? What if she's not really here—just steam and wishful thinking?

But I don't open my eyes. I stay still, letting her touch tether me to something that feels too good to be real.

She slides her hands lower. My breath catches. I groan. She's here—real or not—and I want to believe it.

I try to hold on, but she undoes me with every stroke.

I've waited so long.

I'm terrified I'll say the wrong thing, move too fast, scare her away. But I need her like a drowning man gasps for air.

Her hands press into my hips. I turn around.

There she is. My white shirt soaked through, clinging to her like every version of her I've carried for the past decade.

Her eyes lock on mine—heat and something more.

"Gia, what are you—"

She crashes her lips into mine. Time blurs. Her mouth is soft but fierce, and suddenly we're not in a bathroom—we're everywhere we've ever been, making up for everything we lost.

Her fingers tangle in my hair. I kiss her like I've been starving. Because I have.

Tongues clash. Hands roam. I fist the hem of her shirt, mouth dragging down her neck like I'm trying to memorise her all over again. Like I haven't done it a thousand times in my head.

Fuck, we shouldn't be doing this.

But I'm already gone.

She reaches between my legs and my knees nearly buckle. It's been years. Years of nothing. Of no one. I told myself I was protecting my peace—but really, I just couldn't let anyone in who wasn't her.

And yet here she is. And everything about this feels natural. Right. Like my body never forgot hers.

I spin her around, pin her wrists with one hand, pressing her to the tiles. She arches into me, moaning like she's been wanting this as much as I do.

My hand slips between her thighs. Her panties are soaked. Water or her—I don't care. It's her. It's always been her.

I kiss her neck, that place behind her ear that used to give her goosebumps, then let go of her wrists and drop to my knees.

She gasps when my fingers find her, and I swear I feel her heartbeat in her thighs. I trace her slowly, reverently—a heartfelt apology in a language only her body can understand.

"Charlie," she breathes.

Her voice is my undoing.

My head lowers. My chest heaves. I don't even realise I've frozen until—

"Charlie?" she whispers. She turns. Cups my face with both hands. Her knees brush mine. Her touch, her presence—it's all so soft, so real.

And fuck, she's still here.

I don't deserve it.

But she's here.

And suddenly, it's all too much.

I can't breathe.

The air thickens. My chest locks up, tight and unforgiving. My heart pounds like it's trying to punch its way out.

"Gia," I whisper.

She looks at me like I'm still worth saving. Like I haven't broken every part of this.

It makes it worse.

My thoughts spiral—what if I ruin this? What if I already have?

"Charlie," she says again, softer now. "Talk to me."

But I can't.

I pull back, eyes squeezed shut. Shame crawling up my spine.

My heart thunders.

I can't breathe.

Can't think.

Then—a voice. Bangs.

"Charlie!"

Light. Cold air.

The door crashes open.

Steam curls around her silhouette. Wet hair. My shirt clinging to her like second skin. She's here. Really here.

Her voice cuts through the noise.

"Charlie. Hey—look at me. Are you having a panic attack?"

Fingers wrap around my wrist, warm and firm. And just like that, the world narrows to her.

The heat of her body against mine tugs me back from the edge. I open my eyes. Meet her gaze.

"Breathe with me," she says, calm but firm, like she's done this before. She draws in a slow breath, exaggerated for me to follow. I copy her—inhale through my nose, hold, exhale through my mouth.

Each breath loosens the panic's grip, just a little.

I'm still shaking, still caught in the storm, but I can see her now. Really see her.

I take another breath. Deeper this time. Let myself lean into her touch. Let her warmth sink into my bones.

She reaches over and shuts off the shower. The steady beat of water fades to a slow drip. Silence settles in—just the soft whir of the extractor fan and the ragged thud of my heart.

I slump back against the tiles, breath still shaky, chest still tight—

Then I hear it.

Soft. Off-key. Familiar.

"I've been here before a few times…"

I blink, confused. Gia's kneeling in front of me, soaked to the skin, clutching the ends of her ruined shirt like she doesn't know what to do with her hands.

And then she keeps singing.

"And I'm quite aware we're dying…"

It's rough. Off-key. Barely even a melody.

But fuck, it hits me right in the chest.

She pushes through the chorus of "Always" like it's the only rope left, like if she lets go, we both fall.

And somehow, it's working.

My pulse eases. Breath comes easier.

I huff out a half-laugh. "Are you—are you seriously singing Blink right now?"

She shrugs, soaked hair clinging to her face, water dripping from her lashes. "You used to sing it to me sometimes. With your whole chest. Like you were Tom DeLonge at a sold-out Wembley gig."

I smile despite myself, the memory sucker-punching me in the best way. "God. My horrific Tom DeLonge impression."

"You did the voice and everything," she says, lifting her chin and imitating me in a low, nasal drawl. "Where aarrree youu—"

"—And I'm soo sorry," I finish, barely holding back a laugh.

"See? It helped then. So I figured…" She shrugs, but her voice is quieter now. "I didn't know what else to do."

She tucks a damp strand of hair behind her ear. "You remember the first time I got crossfaded?"

My breath catches somewhere between a laugh and a gasp. "How could I forget? Lambrini and that dodgy weed Nico got off his mate with the ponytail?"

Her nose scrunches. "That was the first and last time I ever mixed that shit. I threw up for, like, five hours. You held my hair while I sobbed into the toilet. I thought I was going to die."

I remember it all. Of course I do. Her, sitting on the bathroom floor in my hoodie, swearing she'd never drink again. My knees going numb against the cold tiles. Her mascara smudged halfway down her face. Me—just desperate to make her feel better.

"And then I sang "Always" until you passed out on the bathroom floor," I say, chest tightening. "It was the only thing I could think to do."

"Exactly," she says softly, moving closer. "So let me do this for you."

I reach out, brushing a stray wet strand of hair from her face, my fingers trembling slightly. "I'm so sorry, G."

She rolls her eyes, her voice sharp but playful. A flash of something—something softer, vulnerable—flickers in her mossy green eyes before she masks it with a smirk. "I swear to god, I'm going to punch you in the face if you keep apologising."

Ah, there she is.

Her hand slides down my arm, grounding me. I swallow hard, suddenly aware. "Shit. I'm so naked right now," I mutter, glancing down at myself.

"As if I haven't seen it all before," she quips, a teasing smile tugging at her lips.

I chuckle, shaking my head. "I think I've grown a couple more hairs on my chest since I was 18, G."

"Only a couple? I'm disappointed," she replies with a smirk, that familiar confident spark in her eyes.

Gia gets up, unhooks the towel from the door, and hands it to me without meeting my gaze. Her eyes flick away from the obvious fact that I'm still very naked, but she's still wearing my soaked white shirt, clinging to her like a second skin—a sight so tempting it feels almost unreal.

"Thanks," I mutter, voice low as I wrap the towel around my waist. I've never felt so exposed—so raw. Maybe this is what I deserve after everything I've put her through.

"Don't mention it," she says softly, but there's concern in her eyes. "Does that... happen a lot?"

Her question catches me off guard. I hesitate, searching for the right words. "More than I'd like to admit," I finally say, my voice raw.

Her expression softens, and for a moment, I brace myself—worried she might see me differently now. But she doesn't pull away. Instead, she moves closer, reaching for my hand. Her presence anchors me, the only thing keeping me steady.

I want to tell her everything, to lay myself bare. But the last thing I want is her pity. I let out a shaky breath. "I think I just need some rest," I say, hoping the half-truth will shift the weight of the moment.

"Yeah, no, of course," she replies, flustered, turning away as if to leave. Then she pauses. "Hey, do you mind if I borrow another t-shirt? I really don't want to leave wearing my clothes from last night." She gestures at the soaked shirt, a small smile tugging at her lips. "And this definitely isn't working for me."

"Who said anything about leaving?" The words slip out before I can stop them—an instinct, maybe a little fear that if she walks out now, I'll lose her again.

She stops, eyebrow raised. "Charlie, you said yourself—you need to rest."

"I do," I admit. "But I want you to stay." My voice drops to a quiet plea.

She's like a bad habit after years of sobriety—dangerous, intoxicating, something I'm not sure I should want. But I can't imagine letting her go. Not now. Not again.

16

GIA

Reinventing Your Exit

I stay with Charlie until he falls asleep—beside him on his bed, crisp white sheets that smell like him, his little crystal collection glinting in the muted light, the curtains half-drawn to keep the sun away.

This is the closest we've been—in every sense of the word—since he came back.

And it scares me.

How easily we've slipped into old comforts. Old motions. Old feelings.

Like he never even left.

Once he's out cold, I head outside, Nico's old bag of weed crinkling in my palm as I sink onto the weathered steps of Charlie's shack. The air smells like salt and woodsmoke. I stare out at the surf. At the skate park we used to haunt as teenagers—Nico, Charlie, and me.

That next generation's out there now, and even from here I can see it—their easy laughter, the way they shove and joke and glow with that untouchable lightness. It tugs at something buried deep inside me.

I open the bag and breathe in the stale weed. It's not potent like it used to be, but it smells like old memories—like the box it's been hidden in. Like Nico's clothes used to smell on his bedroom floor, the morning after he'd spent the night gaming at his mates'. Like indescribable comfort, wrapped in plastic.

And that's good enough.

I tug at the hem of Charlie's oversized T-shirt, watching the waves as they crash against the shore, the salty air mingling with the faint, musty tang of the weed.

A pair of teens catch my eye—maybe fourteen, fifteen at most. The boy's arm is slung casually around the girl's shoulders, but she's glued to her phone. Gen Z romance: screen-lit and distant.

But hey, at least they're outside.

"That stuff will kill you." Charlie's voice cuts through my thoughts. I turn around—and yeah, there it is. The only thing hotter than grey sweatpants on a guy? Grey gym shorts. More specifically: Charlie's tanned, muscular legs in grey gym shorts. That shit should be illegal. Or at least come with a warning.

The sun's starting to set, casting him in soft amber light, illuminating the contours of his face and—annoyingly—making him look even more beautiful.

I scoot over, and he drops down beside me.

His eyes flick to the little bag in my hand. "Wait… is that what I think it is?"

"From Nico's secret stash," I say, holding it up.

Charlie stares at it for a beat. "Gia. Please don't tell me you're seriously thinking about smoking twelve-year-old weed."

I shrug. "Why not? It's vintage."

He lets out a short laugh, disbelieving. "It's compost."

"I mean… it probably won't kill me." I open the bag, take one whiff, and immediately grimace. "Okay, yeah. That smells like regret."

"Yeah, because it is regret. In baggie form."

I seal it shut again and stuff it back into my pocket. "Fine. I'll save it for a special occasion. Like… my midlife crisis."

He bumps his shoulder gently into mine. "You planning on living that long if you keep pulling stunts like this?"

I huff a laugh, but it fades quickly. The air is cooler now, the salt breeze tugging at the ends of my hair.

We sit in silence for a bit, watching the light stretch across the ocean.

My gaze drifts past the surf, back to the two kids at the skate park.

And just like that, I'm somewhere else.

I think about when we used to drink there—Nico, Charlie, and me. I'd always invite myself along, always be the annoying little sister. But Nico and I were so close in age we were basically best friends and worst enemies rolled into one.

Charlie? He always made time for me. Always found a way to be near me. I didn't see it then…

But I do now.

I blink, trying to push the memories away as they come thick and fast—but they cling like smoke, stubborn and sharp.

Charlie stretches his legs out in front of him on the steps. His gym shorts ride low, and for a moment, I'm gone, caught in the way his quads flex beneath tanned skin. But then his expression shifts. And just like that, the weight of the past drops between us like an anchor.

"You don't drink anymore." It slips out—an observation more than a question—but I can't leave it hanging. "Why?"

He doesn't answer right away. Just stares out at the horizon, jaw tight. For a second, I wonder if I've gone too far. Then he sighs.

"Nico used to think I was invincible, didn't he?" He says it like he already knows what's on my mind. He always does. I never have to say a word.

"Invincible and kind of an asshole," I offer, trying to ease the heaviness with a tease—but my chest aches. There's always been truth in our jokes.

Charlie lets out a hollow chuckle. "Yeah, well... I tried to live up to both."

The only sounds between us now are the crash of waves and the distant laughter of kids from the skate park.

Charlie reaches down, picks up a pebble, turns it slowly between his fingers. "I wasn't invincible, G. Not even close." His voice catches. "After Nico died... I fell apart. Drinking, drugs—whatever I could get my hands on. Anything... *everything* to feel nothing."

I ache for him in that moment. All this time, I thought he just left. Moved on. I didn't know he was drowning too—just... in his own way.

"The first time I had a full-blown panic attack, I was at some party on a beach—God knows where. Drunk. High. Completely out of it. Then, out of nowhere, I couldn't breathe. I thought I was dying."

I freeze. I try to picture him like that—but I can't. Charlie was always the calm in the chaos. Cool, collected, untouchable.

"I wish I'd known," I say. I could've helped. But hindsight's a bitch.

Charlie's fingers tighten around the pebble before he tosses it onto the beach below. It ricochets off another with a dull clack. "I don't remember my gap year because I was shitfaced. All the time. I was hurting. And I was lonely. Nico and I were supposed to be travelling together, exploring Aus... but he wasn't there." His voice dips. "He should've been with me."

He swallows hard. "When the year was up, I was too scared to come home. I just... couldn't."

I reach out, laying my hand over his. "You didn't have to handle it alone. You could've called me." My voice catches, the hurt and regret simmering just beneath the surface.

"I know," he whispers, his eyes meeting mine. "I'm sorry. I can't change the choices I made back then, but I want to try now. I want to make things right—with you. With us. I should've come back for you, G."

I don't know how to respond without sounding hurt or resentful, so we sit in silence, watching the water catch the last glimmers of sunlight slipping behind a wall of storm clouds on the horizon.

The truth is, I don't forgive him. Not yet. But something's changed. There's a part of me—small, new—that wants to. A part that didn't exist yesterday. Or a week ago. Or even a month ago.

Every time I fantasised about a moment like this with Charlie, it left me feeling resentful. Bitter I imagined seeing him again, giving him a piece of my mind, tearing into him—hurting him the way he hurt me.

But now? Now, I find myself sitting with his admission, ready—maybe even willing—to let the past go.

Twelve years of anger have left me exhausted, with nothing to show for it. I'm done feeling sorry for myself. Done blaming everyone else.

Above me, the sky darkens—thick with clouds, heavy with rain. The weight of all that anger and resentment turns to water, dissolving into the air.

There's no more hate. No more rage. There just... is.

We're Charlie and Gia. Damned if we do. Damned if we don't.

"I remember," he says, breaking the silence.

I look at him—those ocean-blue eyes, clear as glass, catching the last of the light.

He nods toward the couple at the skate park. "I remember sitting right over there. You and me, at the top of the bowl." A soft smile tugs at his mouth, but it doesn't quite reach his eyes. "You had that awful band tee on. The one you cut up with safety scissors."

I laugh, even though my chest tightens. "I thought I looked cool."

"You did," he says. Quiet. Honest. Like it costs him something to admit it. "Nico had just learned to kickflip. He was showing off, grinning like a little kid." Charlie shakes his head, a soft, sad smile playing at his lips.

The air smells heavy—wet sand and salt—and I feel something shifting between us. A tension without a name, as the past settles in the space between.

"He always made us watch, didn't he? Like we were his personal fan club," he says.

I laugh under my breath. "He was such a show-off."

The first drop falls—a cold splash on the back of my hand. I glance up. The sky's thickening, a dark cloud rolling in fast, swallowing the sunset until everything feels muted, like the world is holding its breath.

"I wasn't watching him, G." More drops scatter at first, speckling the steps between us, leaving tiny craters in the sand. "The entire time... I was always watching you."

The rain comes down in earnest. Heavy. Relentless. Droplets splatter against our clothes, our skin, clinging damp to my cheeks. I should move. We both should. But neither of us does. We just sit there, letting the rain soak in, like it's ours to share. A secret in the downpour.

Charlie looks at me, his eyes dark and soft in the dim light. There's something raw in his gaze, something I haven't seen in years. "All I ever saw was you."

My heart thuds—hard and slow—echoing the way it used to when I was seventeen, curled up in bed, rain pattering against the windows, daring myself to imagine what it would be like to kiss Charlie Andersen.

And now, kissing him is all I can think about.

I feel the warmth of his hand shift, his knuckles grazing mine. For a moment, the rain is all I can hear, all I can feel—dripping down my neck, soaking through my shirt.

The air is thick, heavy—almost suffocating. I glance toward the skate park one last time. They're packing up, rushing out of the rain. The beach is clearing. It's just us. Just us. As if anything else ever mattered.

I look at him, eyes steady, stormy with something I don't have a name for. His breath mingles with the air between us, close enough that I can almost taste the salt on his lips. I turn away, heart racing, but the pull is there—strong and unforgiving. Like a rip current.

"Fuck it," he mutters, voice frayed and low. His hand flies up, fingers curling under my chin, dragging my face back to his. It's not rough—but it's not gentle, either. It's desperate. Like he's been holding back for too long and finally can't anymore.

And then he breaks.

He crashes into me, mouth on mine. The rip current drags me under, stealing the air from my lungs, claiming what's always been his.

The rain is cold, relentless. But his lips are searing. So hot I could drown in them.

And I do.

I close my eyes and let myself melt—let him kiss me the way he always should have. Because let's face it—it was only ever going to be him.

"I need you," he murmurs against my mouth.

He pulls me to my feet, guiding me up, and I follow—without hesitation, without question.

The rain hammers down harder as we stumble up the steps, his hand gripping mine like it's the only thing anchoring him. He drags me toward the open door of his shack, and suddenly we're inside—soaked, breathless, clothes clinging like second skin.

Then I'm up against the wall, hard and fast, my back hitting the plaster, my fingers digging into his shoulders.

His breath is hot against my throat, and I swear I feel it all the way down my spine.

I tug at the hem of his shirt, desperate, greedy. I want more. More of him. More of this. Of us.

But Charlie stops, his forehead pressing against mine, his breath fast and uneven, like he's barely holding himself together. Rain patters against the windows around us—louder now, insistent—echoing the rhythm of my heart. The air between us is thick with heat, cold droplets still sliding down my spine, each one sharp and electric against the warmth of his hands.

He pulls back just enough to look at me, eyes half-lidded, wet lashes clinging together, vulnerability carved into every line of his face.

"Gia," he breathes—low, rough, reverent. Like my name's the only thing holding him together. Then, his voice drops deeper. "Respectfully... take off your fucking clothes."

His thumb traces the curve of my cheek, gentle where everything else feels like a storm. His gaze drifts down my body, slow and aching, before rising to meet mine again—full of heat, full of something that feels dangerously close to love.

"Show me what I've been missing," he growls, voice thick, barely there. "I want what the rest of the world doesn't get to see. Just you and me."

Then he steps back, giving me space—barely an inch, but it feels like a mile. His eyes never leave mine.

My heart pounds as I reach for the hem of my shirt, slipping it off my shoulders and letting it fall to the floor. I'm left in nothing but a borrowed pair of boxer briefs, damp and clinging, but I don't look away.

He watches me like I'm something sacred, taking in every inch. And that's the thing about Charlie Andersen—he's always seen me.

That, I can't deny.

17

GIA

Hands Down

I should turn away. Cover up. Say something to break whatever spell we're under.

I can't.

Instead, I hook my thumbs into my waistband and peel down my underwear, stepping out of it like I didn't hate this man five minutes ago.

"Charlie," I whisper, the sound too soft, too unsure. Too *vulnerable*.

The last time he saw me like this, I was his. The last time he touched me, I shattered.

I hate it.

But right now, I want him to shatter me all over again.

He doesn't move. Just stands there, eye-fucking me like I'm the only woman he's ever laid eyes on. "Touch yourself."

I lift my chin in defiance. "You first."

A challenge. A dare. A little taste of revenge.

His eyes flicker. His mouth curves into that infuriating smirk I know too well. And for a second, I think he's going to call my bluff.

But then—slowly—he reaches for the hem of his shirt, peeling it off in one smooth, deliberate motion.

His gaze locks on mine. "Thirsty, Perelli?"

My pulse stutters.

Holy shit, if that isn't the body of a sinner.

Every ridge of his chest is carved like it was made to ruin me—muscles flexing with the slightest shift, like there's something feral beneath his skin, barely restrained.

A patchwork of ink stretches across his chest and shoulders, and I'm practically salivating. My breathing's gone ragged, shallow. I can't look away.

He dips his hand below his waistband, gripping himself. I can't see it, but I know—he's hard, swollen, probably leaking for me. I imagine how he'd feel in my palm—warm, weighty, pulsing with need.

The thought alone makes my thighs clench. I dig my nails into my palms, fists tight—anything to stop myself from reaching for him.

But it's the tension I crave. The ache. The snap. The surrender.

I slide a hand between my legs.

Charlie's jaw ticks—a flicker of restraint, sharp and involuntary. His eyes darken, locked on mine, tracking every movement like he's tasting it with his gaze.

His forearm flexes, his hand moving faster inside his shorts as his breath hitches.

The tension coils tighter. The heat between us builds—thick, suffocating. Almost unbearable. Almost painful.

Every nerve in me is on fire, responding to the silent demand in his gaze. For a moment, neither of us moves—both caught in the intensity of watching each other. Every breath is shallow. Every inch of space between us, electric.

A flicker of something crosses his face—unease, maybe—but he doesn't break eye contact.

I tilt my head slightly, a silent question in my eyes.

His throat moves as he swallows. No words, but the message is clear; it's been a while.

That vulnerability, barely hidden, throws me off more than any words could.

And yeah, I feel kind of smug about it.

But it doesn't last long.

Soon, we're both lost in it again, suspended in this moment, neither of us daring to close the space between us.

His hand moves slow. Deliberate. Like he knows exactly what he's doing. Eyes locked on mine, trying to worm his way under my skin without a single touch.

Too late. He's already there.

My mouth falls open, breaths shallow and fast, syncing with his as I circle my clit.

We stay caught in the static, eyes locked, tracing every movement the other makes—the way he swallows, thick and deliberate; the way his tongue drags across his bottom lip, slow and sinful. His hair falls forward as he fists himself, his face contorting with pleasure as he watches me.

Each second stretches the tension tighter, thickening the air with unspoken history. But right now, all I can focus on is him. The raw need in his eyes. The way we're sharing this—completely, obscenely intimate—without a single word, a single touch.

And I want him to have this. This version of me no one else gets. The part I never give away—even if it's temporary.

"Fuck yes, like that," I moan, my voice wrecked, as his hand moves faster beneath the fabric. His breaths turn shallow, uneven.

The thought of him coming in his underwear—because of me—turns me on more than I can put into words. It feels like we're teenagers again. That first wild rush of wanting, both of us too afraid to go further.

It's overwhelming.

But it's him.

It's always been him.

And suddenly I feel it again—that same dizzying, heady pull. Like I'm untouched. Inexperienced. Undone by him all over again.

My skin prickles with heat, every nerve alive. I'm so close now—close enough to catch every flicker in his expression. The part of his mouth. The drag of his hand as it speeds up. Lust blazing in his eyes. Jaw tight. Breaths uneven.

A low, raw groan slips out—like he's unravelling, right in front of me.

Then he's there.

His whole body tenses, jerks—release spilling hot and sudden into his underwear.

It's the hottest thing I've ever seen. And it's all for me.

The thought alone tips me over the edge. My climax follows—violent, relentless—fingers trembling as I come undone.

Pleasure crashes through me, sharp and overwhelming, fed by the sight of him still catching his breath, eyes locked on mine.

And for a moment, time stands still.

The rain eases. The static lifts. We're both panting, caught in the afterglow. Until all that's left is the sound of our ragged breathing and the thick heat hanging in the air.

I slump back against the wall, sinking onto the cold wooden floor. My skin's still tingling, soaked and spent. The air's gone quiet—like even time is holding it's breath.

My chest tightens. Suddenly, I feel too bare. Too seen. Like the weight of his gaze might undo me completely.

Without thinking, I reach for the soaked t-shirt I left crumpled on the floor, desperate to cover myself.

"Hey—" Charlie's voice is soft. Warm. Raw.

He takes a step toward me, holding out his own shirt—still damp, but not dripping. "Here. Mine's drier."

For a second, I just stare at it. At him. At the way his fingers curl around the fabric. At the way his jaw tightens, like he's still holding back more than he wants to.

I take the shirt and pull it over my head. It smells like him. Feels like him. Feels like too much and not enough.

"Thanks," I murmur.

He just nods, eyes steady on mine.

But I can't hold his gaze. Not when I feel so exposed. So unmoored. A part of me wants to say something. Another part wants to pretend this was all a dream.

"So... that happened." Charlie says, a small, almost self-conscious smile tugging at the corner of his lips.

I nod, the knot in my chest tightening. "Yeah. It did." My voice is hoarse—not from what just happened, but from the flood of feelings I'm not ready to face yet.

I glance at him again. He hasn't moved—still by the counter, watching me. Waiting.

But it's not pressure. It's quiet understanding. He's letting me set the pace. I just don't know what the pace is anymore.

I don't even know what this was.

All I know is that my head's a mess.

I need time. Space.

I need to get the hell out of here.

"I should go," I say, the words tumbling out before I can stop them. I don't meet his gaze as I pull on his shirt, but I can feel his eyes on me.

Charlie doesn't say anything at first. He nods slowly, a soft, almost reluctant smile tugging at his lips. But beneath it, something flickers—hurt, maybe, or understanding. "Yeah," he says quietly. "Okay."

His shoulders rise with a slow breath, then drop just as slowly. A twitch at the corner of his mouth—like he's about to speak, but swallows it instead.

I gather last night's clothes from where I left them on the back of a chair—the shirt, the tie, the skirt, the fishnets. My chucks are by the door. I don't rush, but I don't look at him again, either.

"I'll see you around." My voice is heavy with everything I'm holding inside. But it's all I can manage—safe, vague. Not a promise, but not a goodbye either.

He nods, eyes lingering on me like he's trying to unravel something just out of reach. Then, quietly, he says, "Take care of yourself, G."

I nod, but it feels like I'm walking away from more than just him.

The cool air hits me as I step outside, and I breathe it in, trying to steady my racing thoughts.

I don't look back.

But my body's still humming with him. And I don't know what that means. All I know is that I need time. And I can't figure it out with him standing there, waiting for an answer.

18

GIA

Swing, Swing

Olive's dragged me to this new bar just outside of town: sleek lines, low lighting, and more men in suits than I can count. The kind of place where the cocktails have their own dress code and the small plates cost more than my Uber, but everything about it screams 'distraction.'

And I sure as hell need a distraction.

Since that unspeakable day with Charlie. I've barely touched my phone, let alone filmed anything. I've lost followers, so now of course she wants content—says it'll "get me back on my game."

She's not wrong—I've been slacking—but my brain's too busy doing overtime, overthinking and overplaying every detail of our mutual solo session to care about 'the game.'

"Take care of yourself, G."

Charlie's words echo in my mind.

What does that even mean? And why did it sound like he was closing a door on this? Whatever this is.

Ugh.

I wanted it to be nothing. But I can't stop thinking about him. Or wanting to do it again.

Shit. I hate myself. Hate how weak I've become over a man. A man I'm supposed to hate, nonetheless.

We grab a booth, and before we've even ordered our drinks, Olive's already talking about the angle she wants. I try to focus, but my mind keeps drifting back to Charlie. His words. The way he looked at me before I left. The way he's somehow still in my head, even while the bartender's doing his best impression of a walking Instagram post.

Hot, yeah. But that's as far as it goes.

That man has ruined me.

"Earth to Gia," Olive says, in that annoying-yet-wise best friend kind of way.

"Sorry, I'm just a little..."

"Distracted?" she finishes, just as the server sets down our cocktails—each one looking like a Pinterest board in a glass.

I nod.

"I noticed." Olive arranges the drinks, snaps a photo, then takes a slow sip. "So... what went down after emo night?"

I fucking knew it.

I take a deep breath, eyes flicking toward my phone, like it might magically offer a way out. But I know I can't avoid this. Not with Olive.

"You want me to lie?" I murmur, my voice sharper than I mean it to be.

Her brow furrows for a beat, but then she leans back, arms folded, watching me. "No. I don't want you to lie. But you've been acting all shady lately, and I can't help but wonder what's going on."

I shift in my seat, fingers tracing the rim of my glass. Charlie's words echo in my head again and again, like a broken record.

"I don't know, Ols. I—" I pause, frustrated with myself. Frustrated with the mess of it all. "We may have had some... I don't even know how to say it without cringing."

"Go on," she says, tone light but expectant.

I groan, cover my face with one hand, then lean in, lowering my voice to a whisper. "We, uh... got each other off. Without getting each other off. If that makes sense."

Olive squints. "As in... you did stuff. With each other. Separately?"

I nod. "But also... not?"

I bite my lip, bracing for her reaction. She just stares, mouth open like I've short-circuited her brain.

Finally, she blinks. "Okay... not what I was expecting."

"You and me both." I let out a breath. "I just... I don't know. After everything, I... God, I don't even know what came over me."

Olive's eyes soften. She uncrosses her arms and leans in. "Hey, you're allowed to feel confused. But you can't keep bottling this up. You've been carrying all this shit around, pretending it doesn't matter."

Her words hit, heavy and right.

I swallow hard, the knot in my chest tightening. "It does matter, though. He's the one who left. And I let him.

And now he's back, and everything feels like it's crashing together. I'm pissed at him. I'm pissed at me. But I'm still—"

"Still what?" Olive asks, voice gentle but steady.

"Still wanting him," I admit, the words tasting foreign in my mouth. "After everything. After he left me behind all those years ago, I'm still—" I swallow hard, trying not to sound as exposed as I feel. "I'm still drawn to him. And I don't know if I'm supposed to hate him or—"

Olive's hand finds mine, her grip warm and steady. "You don't have to figure it all out right now. But you can't keep pretending you're fine when you're not. If you still want him, then let yourself feel it. Whatever it is, it's real. Just don't let it eat you alive."

I nod, her words sinking deep. And for the first time in days, I feel like—maybe—I can finally breathe.

19

CHARLIE

Existentialism on Prom Night

It's been three days since Kitchengate. Three days since I saw her. Heard from her.

I told myself I'd give her space, let her come to me. Big of me, right? Except I've been sat here with my thumb hovering over the DM button like a tragic loser for the last hour. For the third day in a row.

I've written out about ten different messages and deleted every single one. We need to talk. I know that. But I'm being chickenshit about it.

Hey, sorry for losing my head the other night. I don't know if you're pissed off with me or just done, but I really need to talk.

No. Jesus. That's awful. Too much. Way too much.

I try again. Delete it. Again.

She left without slamming the door. That's what gets me. Just closed it, quiet. Like she didn't even want the last word. Like she'd already said enough without saying anything.

And I just let her go. Didn't fight for it. Didn't chase her. Just stood there like a dickhead.

Christ, I'm such a knob. A clueless, gutless, fucking knob.

I sit back in my chair, running a hand through my hair. My mind's spinning, and I can feel my anxiety creeping back in. Maybe I need to ground myself. I've been meditating more lately—mostly to avoid panicking about the fact that I'm back here, in the same town, dealing with feelings I thought I buried years ago.

I grab the small lepidolite crystal on my shelf and roll it in my hand, taking a slow, deep breath. Focus on the present, I tell myself. Stay grounded. Be calm. Be patient. Feel the feelings. Let them go.

I try to clear my mind, but all I can think about is Gia. The way we practically fucked without even touching. The way she came. The way she left...

God... how many years has it been?

I'm about to close my eyes and let my mind go quiet when my phone pings. I pick it up, and my pulse speeds up as I see Gia's name.

Gia: Hey

I stare at the screen, wondering if I've somehow manifested this. That maybe, just maybe, the universe is finally rooting for me. For this. For us.

My heart stutters. It's a single word, but it feels like a floodgate. She's reached out. I don't know if I'm relieved or more nervous than before.

I swallow hard and quickly type back, my fingers shaking.

Charlie: Hey

There's a long pause before she replies, and for a split second, I wonder if she's been drinking.

Gia: I've been thinking about the other day...

I sit up straighter, my fingers gripping the phone tighter. There's something in her words that sounds off. She's not angry, but she's not sounding like herself either.

Charlie: Me too

My thumb hovers over the screen again, but this time, it's because I'm waiting for the next message. I have no idea what she's going to say, but the fact that she's even texting me at all makes me feel like there's hope.

Gia: So...

She pauses. I feel a shift in the air, like she's building up to something.

Gia: I may be a little drunk

I can't help but chuckle, even though I know this could go either way.

Charlie: How drunk?

Gia: Drunk enough to text you. I don't know if that's a good idea, but here I am

I lean back, a slight grin on my face.

Charlie: I'm glad you did

Gia: Me too. I think

Charlie: Where are you?

Gia: Ember & Ivy. It's a little pretentious, but the cocktails are good

Charlie: A little too good, by the sound of it

I wait for the next message, my breath caught in my chest. For all the mistakes I've made, maybe this is the chance I need to make things right. Maybe she's ready to talk. Hell, maybe she's ready to be real with me for once.

Gia: Olive's abandoned me. She's flirting with the hot bartender

I can't help the grin that spreads across my face.

Charlie: Oh? A hot bartender, you say? You didn't think to flirt with him yourself?

Gia: Believe me, Olive's doing enough flirting for the both of us

I chuckle, feeling that tension in my chest start to ease.

Charlie: Well, if you need someone to swoop in and be your fake boyfriend for the night, I'm only a text away

Gia: You'd make a terrible fake boyfriend

Charlie: Ouch

My ego

Another pause, longer this time, and I wait, fingers hovering over the keyboard.

Gia: I'm sorry. I don't even know why I'm talking to you right now… okay, actually I do

I bite back a grin. The way she's messaging me—looser, a little braver—makes my chest ache in that ridiculous, hopeful way I've been trying to ignore.

Charlie: So why are you, then?

There's a long pause. I hold my breath, waiting.

Gia: Because I don't know what any of this means, and it's messing with my head

I read it over a few times, feeling that pull in my chest tighten, like she's handed me something fragile. And maybe, for the first time, we're both ready to face what this is.

Charlie: G... you're not the only one

I watch as the typing bubble appears, then disappears. Then appears again. My pulse quickens, hanging onto whatever comes next. But nothing does.

I hover over the keyboard, fingers twitching, my heart pounding before I finally type:

Charlie: Want me to come rescue you?

The bubble comes back almost instantly this time.

Gia: Define rescue

I smile, shaking my head.

Charlie: Well, I'm no bartender, but I am a hot chef. I could swing by, whisk you away, and feed you something better than overpriced small plates

Her reply is immediate.

Gia: Cocky much?

Charlie: Always

Another pause, and I swear I'm holding my breath again.

Gia: Fine. But don't make it weird

I grin, already grabbing my keys, then reply.

Charlie: Famous last words, Perelli

"This is hands down the best thing I've ever had in my mouth," Gia says, wiping ketchup from the corner of her lips.

She's perched on my kitchen counter, halfway through a dirty smashburger and still somehow managing to look like she's flirting on purpose. I lean opposite her, arms crossed, trying not to stare like a man possessed. Or obsessed. Either way, I've got it bad.

"Careful, G. That sort of talk's easily misconstrued," I say, brow raised.

"I know," she smirks, eyes glinting.

"Smart mouth," I murmur, taking the bait anyway.

Her smirk deepens as she licks her thumb, slow and deliberate. "You love it."

Yeah. I really fucking do.

She's playing with fire—and fuck me, she knows exactly what she's doing. I'd whipped up my signature junk food classic: double plant-based patties, vegan American cheese, gherkins, relish, mustard, lettuce. Messy as hell. And she's devouring it like it's the second coming.

Still, she's not just eating—she's watching me while she does it. Like she's chewing on her next line, waiting to see how much more she can push.

She polishes off the last bite, letting out a soft groan of satisfaction as she wipes her hands with a napkin. "You've officially ruined junk food for me, Charlie. I'm never going to want takeout again."

"Just doing my job," I say with a grin, setting another glass of water in front of her.

She takes a sip before hopping off the counter, her movements a little unsteady. I'm already halfway to reaching out when she steadies herself. "I'm good, I'm good," she says, waving me off with a laugh. "Just a little burger drunk."

"Burger drunk." I chuckle. "Is that a thing now?"

"Feels like it." She tosses her napkin in the bin and heads to the sink with her plate. I let her. I like how at home she is here. "I've gotta head out," she says over her shoulder. "Got a sponsor thing tomorrow—powdered oat milk." She pulls a face, then sighs. "Need to come up with some recipes for it."

I cross my arms, leaning casually against the counter. "Powdered oat milk? Seriously?"

"Yeah, glamourous, right?" she says dryly, running a hand through her hair. "But it pays the bills, so here we are."

"Need some help with that?" The words come out before I can stop them.

Her eyes narrow playfully. "With powdered oat milk?"

"Sure." I shrug, playing it cool. "I've got a few ideas rattling around. I could make it... less powdered oat milk-y."

She hesitates, her lips twitching as she considers it. "I don't know, Charlie. You've already done too much tonight. I can't keep roping you into my messes."

"Hey," I say, stepping closer, my tone soft but insistent. "I'm offering. Besides, I owe you one after... well, everything. Cleaning up messes is kinda my thing these days."

She pauses, something flickering in her expression—like she's not sure whether to let me carry the weight of that or deflect it. Her gaze softens, and for a second, it feels like the moment might tip into something heavier.

But then she blinks, smirks. "You really think you can make powdered oat milk sexy?"

I let the corner of my mouth curl, slow and deliberate. "Oh, for sure. I'll have you begging for it."

Her breath catches—just barely—but enough. A flush rises in her cheeks, though she covers it with a laugh, shaking her head like I'm trouble and she knows it.

"You're honestly like the chef version of… you know, a gentleman in the streets and a freak in the sheets."

I blink, caught off guard. She's watching me now, eyes dancing, but there's heat behind it. Challenge. Curiosity.

I huff a laugh, scratching the back of my neck. "That's one way to put it."

"No, I'm serious," she says, leaning forward and wagging a finger at me. That's when it hits me—she's properly drunk. Like, can't make a good decision drunk. And that means tonight? Nothing's happening. No matter how much I want it to.

"You've got this whole 'artiste in the kitchen' vibe going on," she slurs a little, "but then you turn around and make the best junk food I've ever had. It's… dangerous."

"Dangerous?" I echo, raising an eyebrow, trying not to let my voice get too low.

She nods, grinning. "Because now I know you can do both. You're the guy who can serve up kale smoothies *and* double smashburgers without breaking a sweat. That's rare."

I shake my head, chuckling, the corner of my mouth tugging up. "Finish your water, G. Can't have you turning into a puddle before the night's even over."

"Yes, Chef," she says with a wink, leaning back against the counter like she's perfectly comfortable here.

I head to the sink, grabbing a dish towel to busy my hands. This game we're playing? It's dangerous. But I can't seem to stop.

Gia's phone pings, the sound sharp and unwelcome against the comfortable quiet. She glances down at it and sighs. "Oh, that's my Uber," she says, tucking her phone back into her bag.

I turn, leaning against the counter. "You ordered a taxi?"

She shrugs, sliding the strap of her bag over her shoulder. "What, you thought I was going to let you drive me home after everything you've done already? You've played chef, bartender, and host tonight. I'm not adding chauffeur to your list."

"I don't mind," I say, crossing my arms. "You shouldn't be heading home alone this late."

She raises an eyebrow, that smirk of hers back in full force. "Charlie, I've been heading home alone for years. I think I can handle it."

I step closer, letting the towel drape over the counter. "I know you can. But it doesn't mean you should have to."

Her expression softens for just a second before she shakes her head, a playful grin breaking through. "Relax, Chef. I'm a big girl. And besides, my ride's already here."

I watch as she adjusts her bag, pulling her hair to one side. "Well, at least let me walk you out."

"You're not going to take no for an answer, are you?"

"Never."

She laughs, and it's warm and genuine, cutting through the tension that's been building between us. "Alright, come on, then."

I grab my keys out of habit and follow her to the door. The cool night air hits us as we step outside, her taxi already waiting at the curb.

Gia turns to me, and for a moment, it's like time stretches. She lingers, her eyes meeting mine, and I think she's about to say something. But instead, she just smiles, soft and sincere. "Thanks, Charlie. For everything."

"Anytime," I reply, my voice low. "Let me know when you get home."

She hesitates, like she's waiting for me to say more, before finally slipping into the back seat of the taxi. I watch as it pulls away, the glow of the taillights disappearing down the street.

I stand there for a moment longer, the quiet settling back in around me. This game we're playing? It's not just dangerous—it's addictive. And I'm not sure how much longer I can keep myself from breaking the rules.

20

GIA

I Caught Fire

Charlie: So, I've been brainstorming some oat milk recipes...

Gia: Ooh, I'm intrigued

Hit me with it, Chef

Charlie: To start: creamy oat milk soup. Maybe cucumber and dill. Refreshing, perfect for summer

Gia: Immediately no. Cold soup is just a smoothie trying too hard. Next

Charlie: Lol, noted. How about vegan oat milk pasta primavera? Creamy sauce, fresh peas, asparagus, lemon zest...

Gia: Hmm. Losing me at creamy. What else you got?

Charlie: Wow, tough crowd...

Okay... what about strawberry shortcake? Fluffy biscuits, fresh strawberries, and whipped cream. All plant-based of course

Gia: Now you're speaking my language. Do you mind picking up the ingredients? My head hurts

Charlie: Already packed. But you're helping

Gia: Supervising is helping

Charlie: Classic. Blame the alcohol you didn't have to drink. Get your apron ready. I'll be there in an hour

I lean back in my seat, cradling the mug of coffee I've just made with the powdered oat milk. I sigh dramatically. The hangover's real, but this coffee? Not so much.

Just as I take another sad sip, a notification pops up on my phone from the door camera—it's Charlie. I get up to answer, still cradling the mug. As I open the door, there he stands, balancing two bags in one hand and a coffee carrier in the other, housing two takeaway cups. He steps inside with a grin, his eyes flicking to the mug.

"Please tell me one of those is for me," I say, eyeing the freshly brewed coffee.

"Instant not hitting the spot?"

He doesn't even have to ask.

"Not with a raging hangover."

Charlie grins, shaking his head, as he follows me through to the kitchen.

He sets one of the bags down on the island with a dramatic thud. "Ingredients," he says with a grin, before handing me the second bag directly. "And this one's for your raging hangover," he says, exaggerating the last two words.

I dive into the second bag, eagerly sifting through a multitude of snacks. There's a bar of vegan caramel chocolate, a green smoothie, a selection of sweets, a giant bag of crisps, and—wait—two gooey sticky cinnamon buns wrapped up carefully in foil. My mouth waters at the sight.

I look up, narrowing my eyes playfully. "Did you make these?"

"Yeah," he mutters, though his tone's a little too casual. "Had some time on my hands... figured you might like something homemade."

I raise an eyebrow, sensing there's more to that than he's letting on, but I don't press it. "Well, lucky for you, I'm a sucker for cinnamon buns." I tear into one, the warm, sticky sweetness of cinnamon hitting my senses. It's perfect. "Mm. I've died and gone to cinnamon bun heaven."

He barks out a laugh, shaking his head. "Worth smuggling my seven-year-old sourdough starter into the country, then—I'll take it. But be careful throwing compliments around, G. I might start thinking you actually like me."

I shoot him a pointed look, then glance at the coffee, the snacks, then back up at him. My gaze softens. "I think this might be the most thoughtful thing anyone's ever done for me."

"Your expectations must be ridiculously low, then."

"Something like that," I say.

"Well, it's been a while. I figured you'd have some kind of hangover craving—just wasn't sure if you were a sweet or savoury girl these days."

I shoot him a pointed look. "I'm an everything girl. Sweet, sour, salty, bitter, umami… disgustingly healthy, disgustingly greasy. Give me all of it."

Charlie chuckles, leaning back against the counter, just… watching me.

I take another bite, not even bothering to hide the way I'm stuffing my face. "Seriously, what's in this? Crack?" I glance up at him, amused.

"Crack, and an ungodly amount of sugar."

I try my hardest to stop my eyes rolling back. "Whatever it is, I want to bathe in it."

The low rumble of his laugh does something it definitely shouldn't in my current state. When he shifts his weight, folding his arms, my eyes betray me, snagging on the sinew of his biceps. Here comes the hangover horn. Fantastic. Just what I need.

I force myself to look back down at my coffee, trying to focus. "Well, you did make me the best burger, and now the best cinnamon bun of my life. So, I guess you've earned it."

"Oh, I'm aware." There's something warm and teasing in his gaze, but there's something else, too. Something heavier.

For a moment, the kitchen feels smaller, the air thick. I clear my throat, trying to shake off the moment before it swallows me whole. "So, what do you need to me to do? With the shortcake, I mean? I've never made them before."

Charlie grins, eyes lighting up. "Don't worry, I'll handle the shortcake."

"You sure about that, Chef?" I smirk. "Last time we made biscuits together you almost burned down your kitchen."

"I'm never going to live that down, am I?" He pauses, his gaze landing on the bag full of ingredients.

"I don't let things go that easily, Charlie," I say, picking up the mixing bowl and shooting him a sly look over my shoulder. "But it's probably best if you make the shortcakes. I'll handle the cream."

"That's what she said," he chuckles, smug and unrepentant.

"Oh no you did *not*." I groan, torn between laughter and dying of second-hand embarrassment.

"I absolutely did." His grin is wicked, and it only makes it worse.

My cheeks burn, the flush crawling all the way down my neck, and I duck my head, pretending to focus on the groceries just to escape his gaze. I rummage through the bag with more energy than necessary, trying to ignore the way my heart skips in my chest.

"Where's the coconut milk?" I ask, frowning as I pull out a punnet of strawberries and a bag of sugar.

"We don't need coconut milk."

I glance up, narrowing my eyes. "How am I supposed to make cream with no coconut milk?"

He shrugs, a mischievous grin tugging at his lips as he leans casually against the counter. "I figured we'd experiment—use the powdered oat milk instead. If it's a disaster, then we'll just wing it."

"Because that's worked out so well in the past," I say, cocking an eyebrow as I cross my arms over my chest. "Look at you, overruling my decisions. Is this your kitchen takeover? Should I be worried about my content?"

His grin widens. "Maybe you should. Could be the start of my influencer career. Oat milk chef extraordinaire."

"I mean, now you mention it, you could totally be one of those thirst-trap chefs I see all over TikTok and Instagram. *Oat Milk Daddy* does have a certain ring to it, don't you think?"

Did I seriously just say that?

Gia. Stop. Flirting.

"Move over, *Sourdough Whisperer*, or whatever his name is." Charlie chuckles, sliding the scales toward him as he measures the flour into a bowl. "Don't worry, boss. I know better than to step on your brand. Think of it as a collaboration... featuring *Oat Milk Daddy*."

I burst out laughing, covering my face with my hands. "Stop. I'm cringing so hard I might combust."

Charlie smirks, clearly enjoying himself. "What? I think it's got potential. *Oat Milk Daddy*: chef, heartthrob, content creator. I can see the merch already."

I groan, grabbing a handful of flour and threatening to toss it at him. "Keep going, and this collaboration is over before it starts."

He raises his hands in mock surrender, a grin still plastered on his face. "Alright, alright. I'll save it for my solo career."

I roll my eyes, though I can't help the smile tugging at my lips. "Well, you might want to focus on *this* collaboration if you want to keep your reputation intact." I grab the measuring cup and start sifting the flour. "Now, let's make this shortcake something worthy of the content gods, yeah?"

We get to work, falling into a rhythm of measuring, pouring, sieving, stirring...

I can't help but glance at him, his hands moving confidently, his focus sharp. It's like he's been in my kitchen a hundred times already. Maybe it's the familiarity, or maybe it's just the way he makes everything look so damn easy. Either way, there's something oddly comforting about the way he works—the way he hums under his breath, the casual ease in his movements. It's the kind of thing that could make you forget everything else for a little while.

"So," he says, his voice cutting through the quiet clatter of bowls and spoons, "are we going to talk about the elephant in the room?"

I freeze mid-stir, my heart tripping over itself. "There's... an elephant in here?" I mutter, eyes fixed on the batter like it might save me. Deflecting. Obviously.

He lets out a breathy laugh, not quite meeting my eyes. "You know. The part where we both had a little... solo moment in my kitchen the other day?"

The air shifts. Thicker now. My cheeks burn and I suddenly find the mixing bowl very interesting.

"I don't know what you're talking about," I say, my voice a little too tight, a little too fast.

His smirk falters for a split second. Then he leans in, slow and deliberate, his breath ghosting across my cheek. "Oh? Funny how you seem to have forgotten the most memorable part of the day."

He pauses, the air between us tightening like a wire pulled taut.

I lean in too, closing the space just enough to feel the heat of him. "Hm. I tend to forget small, insignificant details."

"Ouch," he says, clutching his chest. His voice is light, but there's a flicker—something darker, hungrier—beneath the surface. His eyes drop to my lips, just for a second, then back up to meet mine.

And that unspoken question? It lingers—loud, hot, and impossible to ignore.

"What's the matter, Chef?" I step closer, almost daring him, the space between us narrowing. My voice lowers to a teasing whisper, sharp and playful. "Can't handle the heat?" My breath catches as I lean in just a fraction more. "Well, you know what they say about that."

His smirk twists into something more knowing, dangerous even, and he holds my gaze, the challenge clear in his eyes. He doesn't back away. Instead, he inches closer, his breath brushing against my cheek as he mutters, "I can handle a lot more than you think."

The words hang in the air, hot and heavy, and my heart races a little faster than I want to admit.

Time stands still, the world around us fading into the background as the distance between us shrinks to nothing. The only thing that matters now is the magnetic pull between us—raw, undeniable. My heart is pounding, the air thick with anticipation.

I barely breathe as his hand shifts, the slight brush of his fingers against mine sending a shiver down my spine. The space between us hums, charged with something unspoken, something that feels too dangerous to ignore. His eyes stay locked on mine, daring me to make the next move, yet I can't seem to pull away.

It's as if the universe has decided this is the moment—the moment where everything else falls away and only the tension remains.

"Gia..." His voice is low. A warning. And it sends a rush of heat through me, straight between my legs.

I could kiss him. I could pull him to me right now, and there would be no going back. But for some reason, I wait. I want to see if he'll break first, if he'll make that final move.

His lips are on mine before I can even process what's happening. It's not gentle, not tentative. It's hungry, fierce, like we've both been holding back for far too long. His tongue demands entrance, and I give it, matching his intensity with a hunger of my own.

His hand slides to my waist, pulling me into him with a force that takes my breath away. The heat of his body presses against mine, and I feel every inch of him—his chest, his breath, the undeniable tension between us.

The kitchen fades. The dough, the ingredients, the camera—none of it matters anymore. It's just us, lost in the kiss, in the moment, in the rush of what we both know is inevitable.

I'm not backing down. And neither is he.

21

CHARLIE

Don't Wait

Drowning. I'm fucking drowning here. Every kiss, every touch pulls me under—but I refuse to break for air.

My hands roam her body, mapping every curve like muscle memory. Like I've been chasing this forever. Maybe I have. Maybe that's why I can't stop. Why I haven't told her everything. Not now. Not when I finally have her like this.

Her lips part against mine, soft and insistent, and the sound she makes—the softest, breathiest moan—sends a jolt straight to my cock. Her hands are in my hair, tugging just enough to make me groan. She moves closer, and when her hips press against me, all reason disappears.

"Charlie," she murmurs against my mouth, her voice low and shaky, like she's barely holding it together. Her hands slide down my chest, her nails catching on the fabric of my shirt, and then she tugs at it. "Why is this still on?"

Fuck. This woman will be the death of me. I grab the hem and strip it off, her gaze tracking every inch of bare skin.

Before I can overthink it, she takes my hand and leads me toward the sofa. It's only a few steps, but each one feels loaded, my pulse ticking up with every inch we close. I follow—because how the hell could I not?

Then, with a wicked little smirk, she shoves me down.

I land hard, back hitting the cushions, feet planted on the floor—just in time for her to climb into my lap, straddling me like she owns every part of me.

She does.

Her hips roll, slow and purposeful, and I have to bite back the groan that rises in my throat. Every shift of her body against mine is maddening, dragging me closer to the edge.

"You're killing me, G," I rasp.

She just grins. "Then stop holding back."

It's a challenge. A dare. One I couldn't resist even if I tried.

Her lips graze my jaw, then my neck—soft touches that send a shiver racing down my spine. She shifts again, slow, with purpose, rocking against me. The friction knocks the breath from my lungs. I'm losing my grip—on my resolve, on everything but her.

I press my feet into the floor, trying to ground myself in this moment—this moment I've replayed in my head a thousand times. Her eyes find mine, dark with want... and something else I can't quite name. And suddenly, the world narrows. It's just us. The way it always should have been.

She leans in, close enough for her breath to dance across my lips. But she doesn't kiss me. My hands slide to her waist, pulling her closer, and she lets out a soft gasp as her body melts into mine, like we were always meant to fit this way. Her movements grow more deliberate—slow at first, then faster, chasing something just out of reach. Every roll of her hips, every breathy sound she makes, sends me spiralling further out of control.

"Gia..." Her name leaves my mouth like a prayer, a warning, low and broken, but she doesn't stop. Her lips brush my ear. Her fingers tighten on my shoulders, holding on as if she feels it too—everything unravelling.

And just like that, I'm gone. Completely, blissfully, and willingly undone.

"Gia—"

"Tell me to stop," she whispers, her mouth at my jaw, her breath hot against my skin. "If you really want me to, I will."

Her hands are in my hair again, tugging just hard enough to scatter every thought that isn't her. I pull back slightly—just enough to breathe—and press my forehead to hers.

"No," I murmur, voice low and ragged. "Don't stop." My hands slide down the curve of her back, fingers digging in just enough to let her feel it—that need, that ache. They find her hips, and I hold on tight, grounding myself in her, in this moment, trying not to come undone completely. "Don't ever fucking stop."

Her breath catches, and her body answers—moving in a slow, torturous rhythm that drives me feral. I can't look away. Her lips part, her eyes flutter, her face twists in pleasure—and it's the most breathtaking thing I've ever seen.

"Fuck." The word punches out of me, unbidden, as she grinds against me—slow, deliberate, unhurried—her eyes locked on mine. I'm torn in two. Part of me wants to let my eyes slip shut, to lose myself in the sensation. But I can't. I need to see her. Need to watch her fall apart.

My head tips back, just enough to breathe, but my gaze stays fixed on her. Her lips find my neck, grazing heat over skin, then trace along my jaw—each touch sending lightning straight through me. This time, the groan escapes, low and rough and utterly beyond my control.

"Charlie," she breathes, and it's a plea and a promise all at once. "Come with me."

Her voice is soft—almost reverent—but the roll of her hips is anything but. Every shift steals a little more of my control, until all that's left is her.

Her breath hitches—sharp, quiet—a sound that slices through me like lightning. She clings to me, nails digging into my shoulders, her body trembling, tightening, teetering right on the edge.

"Gia," I groan, my hands locking onto her hips, guiding her as my own release barrels toward me—fast, relentless, impossible to hold back. "Fuck."

Her head tips back, lips parting on a soft, broken cry that shatters me. The sight of her coming undone pulls me under, and I let go.

My body jerks, muscles taut, cock throbbing, balls tight as the wave crashes over me. I spill into my briefs, stars bursting behind my eyes, every nerve on fire, every thought obliterated by her.

And then, for a moment, the world holds its breath.

Everything stills. Quiet. Weightless. And all I feel is her—this soft, trembling, perfect woman wrapped in my arms. Her skin is flushed, radiant with the afterglow, warm against mine. Her scent clings to me. Her taste lingers on my tongue.

She's everything.

She's always *been* everything.

And she always will be.

Please, I beg the universe in silence. *Let me have this. Let me drown in her.*

But the weight of what I haven't told her settles over me like a stone, heavy and cold, threatening to crush the perfect moment we've just shared. I don't know if it's guilt, shame, or something darker that makes the words catch in my throat—but they do.

Still, I push through.

Because after everything I've done—everything I've put her through—she deserves the truth. No more hiding. No more silence.

Just her. And everything I've been too much of a coward to say.

She lifts her head from my shoulder, eyes wide, still sparkling with mischief—until something shifts. The light dims, replaced by quiet concern.

"Are you okay?" she asks, propping herself up, searching my face.

I should be the one asking her that. I should be checking in on her.

But I guess I've always been selfish like that.

"Gia, there's... something I haven't told you," I say, my voice rougher than I mean it to be. The weight of it sits heavy on my chest, pressing tighter with every beat of silence. "And I know this might not be the right time, but I can't keep pretending it's not there."

Her smile falters, replaced by a wary stillness as her eyes lock on mine. Wide. Searching. Bracing.

"Okay... why do I feel like you're about to tell me you're married with five kids or something?"

I shake my head quickly. "No. It's nothing like that."

"Alright," she says, voice calm, steady—but her eyes betray her. There's a flicker there, sharp and fleeting. Fear, maybe. Like she's preparing for the worst. "Whatever it is... you can talk to me."

But the way she looks at me—like she's ready to be gutted—twists the knife in my chest.

I shift beneath her, throat thick, fingers curling into the hem of her shirt like it's the only thing keeping me grounded. I have to tell her. I've avoided it for too long. And it's eating me alive.

"Okay... so the thing is," I start, voice tight, trying to steady myself, "I haven't really... buttered anyone's muffin for a while."

I flash a small, self-deprecating smirk, hoping to diffuse the tension, but the weight of the truth presses down harder than ever.

She squints at me. "Was that a *Mean Girls* reference?"

I give a little shrug. "What can I say? Glen Coco raised my standards."

She blinks, lips twitching—caught between laughing and letting her concern take over. Then, something shifts in her eyes—a flicker of recognition.

"But… I know this. The other day, in the kitchen… you had this look. I kinda put two and two together, but…" Her voice trails off as she studies me. "Charlie? How long is 'a while'?"

The question lands like a soft punch to my gut—her tone a mix of curiosity and something else I can't quite name. I feel the weight of her attention pressing down, and I know there's no dodging this.

I hesitate, her steady gaze pulling the words out of me. "Nine years," I say finally.

Her brow furrows, confusion and disbelief flickering across her face. "Nine years?" she echoes softly, as if trying to make sense of it.

I nod, still gripping the hem of her shirt. "It was around the same time I quit drinking. Stopped the drugs. I was in a bad place, G. Real bad. Cutting everything out—it wasn't just about staying sober. It was about resetting everything. Including…" My voice falters, but I force the words out. "Including sex."

She doesn't speak. Doesn't move. But her expression shifts—shock, curiosity, and something softer I can't quite place.

"It took me a long time to even figure out who I was without all that stuff," I admit, my voice dropping quieter now. "And even longer to start feeling like myself again. But… I got there. Slowly. Piece by piece."

Her lips part slightly, eyes searching mine like she's seeing something new, something unexpected. "So you just… decided to stop?"

I let out a small, humourless laugh. "It wasn't some grand plan. At first, I just didn't trust myself. Didn't want to drag anyone into the mess I was in. But then it became more than that—a way to stay grounded. A way to prove I could stick to something when everything else was falling apart."

She's quiet for a moment, her fingers brushing against mine like she's anchoring herself to me. "And now?" she asks, voice careful but gentle.

"Now," I say, locking eyes with her, "I know who I am again. And I know what I want." My voice falters. "I'm not afraid to want it anymore."

Her eyes soften, the flicker of surprise melting into something warmer. "Nine years," she murmurs, shaking her head slightly. "That's... wow."

I let out a nervous laugh. "Yeah, not exactly a stellar way to impress someone."

She cracks a smile, fingers curling over mine. "No, but it does explain why you're so obsessed with your damn sourdough starter."

The tension breaks, and I laugh—lighter than I have in a long time. Trust Gia to tease me and put me at ease, all in the same breath.

"I'm glad you told me," Gia says softly, her voice steady. There's something in it I can't quite place—concern, maybe, or a quiet fear. She shifts closer, her hand resting lightly on my chest. "Wait... have I crossed a boundary? I didn't mean to make you do anything you didn't want to."

Her words hit me like a gut punch. I shake my head quickly. "G, no," I say firmly, covering her hand with mine. "You didn't make me do anything. Everything we've done—it's because I wanted to. Because I want you."

She watches me, lips pressed together, uncertainty flickering in her eyes. "But you've spent years being intentional about everything. About what you let into your life. What if I messed that up for you?"

"You didn't mess anything up," I say, my voice low but steady. "If anything, you reminded me what it feels like to actually live again. To want something—someone—so much it scares the hell out of me. Being with you doesn't feel like losing control, Gia. It feels like finding it."

Her expression softens, her shoulders relaxing just a fraction. "You're sure?" she asks, voice barely above a whisper.

I smile, gently tucking a strand of hair behind her ear. "I've never been more sure of anything in my life."

Her voice drops even quieter, but the question lands like a thunderclap.

"What happens when you go back to Aus?" she asks, fingers nervously fiddling with the hem of her shirt, eyes dropping to her lap.

My chest tightens. The weight of her words settles like a stone in my gut. I knew this moment was coming—I just didn't expect it now, with us tangled together, her warmth still lingering on my skin.

"I don't know," I admit, voice low. "I've been trying not to think that far ahead."

Her eyes lift, searching my face for something I'm not sure I can give. "Not thinking about it doesn't make it go away, Charlie," she says, steady but raw. "You can't just avoid it forever."

"I know," I say, running a hand through my hair. "But Gia, the idea of leaving... walking away from this—from you—it feels impossible. I can't even wrap my head around it."

She exhales slowly, fingers still fidgeting. "But that's the plan, isn't it? The residency ends, and then you go back to Australia."

"It *was* the plan," I say, emphasising the past tense, hoping she catches it. "Before I came back here. Before you."

She blinks, lips parting like she wants to say something, but no words come. For a moment, the air between us is thick with unspoken possibilities—the kind that terrify me because they feel so damn real.

"I don't know what I'm doing yet, Gia," I continue, voice soft but steady. "All I know is I don't want to lose this. I don't want to lose you."

Her lips press into a thin line, eyes glistening with unshed tears. "Charlie, I don't want to lose this either," she says finally, voice cracking a little. "But I don't know how to do this if there's an expiration date hanging over us."

I reach for her hand, holding it tight. "Then let's figure it out together," I say, voice firm. "I'm not going anywhere without a fight, Gia. I need you to know that."

She looks at me, brows knitting as she searches my face—maybe for reassurance, maybe for hope.

"Okay," she says softly, the word fragile, like it could shatter with the slightest wrong move.

It's not a resolution. Not yet. But it's a step. And for now, that has to be enough.

22

GIA

The Middle

"Celibate? As in..." Olive's mouth hangs open. The fact that she's speechless speaks volumes.

I wince, sinking further into the plush corner of Olive's sofa.

"Hold on a sec. You expect me to believe that a guy who looks like that—the guy who's been eye-fucking you freely in front of me every time you're in a room together doesn't have sex? Like, ever?"

The fluffy throw pillow I'm clutching feels like my only shield against her incredulous tone. Across from me, she's perched on the edge of the armchair, legs tucked under her, her face frozen in a mix of disbelief and amusement.

"Shh! Can you not broadcast it to the entire neighbourhood?" I whisper-yell, darting a glance at the open windows.

Olive raises her hands in mock surrender, a smirk tugging at her lips. "Sorry, didn't know I was spilling the week's hottest tea."

I groan, burying my face in the pillow for a second. When I resurface, she's still grinning, waiting for me to explain. "It's not what you think," I start, fidgeting with the fringe on the pillow.

Her eyebrows lift. "It's not what I think? Gia, you just told me the guy you're into hasn't done... anything in years. And now I'm supposed to... what? Pretend like that's not the most surprising thing I've heard all week?"

"It's not like we had sex!" I blurt out, my cheeks immediately heating. "We didn't even get close to that."

"Oh?" Olive leans forward, her smirk deepening. "Then what exactly did you two get close to?"

I groan again, this time throwing the pillow onto the floor. "We made out, okay? Things got... heated. But we didn't, you know, do it." My hands make vague gestures, and Olive snickers.

"Gia Perelli... did you dry hump Charlie the chef?" she teases, her tone dripping with playful shock.

"Oh my God, stop," I mutter, covering my face with my hands.

She laughs, the sound warm and infectious, but when it tapers off, her tone softens. "Okay, okay. So... what's the deal? What happens now?"

I sigh, letting my hands fall to my lap. Sunlight casts a soft warmth across the room, but I still feel like I'm under a spotlight. "Honestly? I have no idea. I'm out of my depth, Ols. I don't know what any of this means. He's been... was... celibate for like nine years."

Olive's eyebrows shoot up again. "Nine years? Damn. That's..." She pauses, searching for the right word.

"A lot," I supply, running a hand through my hair. "And he told me it wasn't just about sex. It was everything—drinking, partying, the whole downward spiral. He said stopping all of it was the only way he could find himself again."

Olive tilts her head, her teasing smile fading into something softer. "That's kind of huge, G. I mean, good for him for being that self-aware."

I nod, my throat tightening. "Yeah. It's just... I'm worried."

"About what?"

"What if I pushed him too far? What if I made him do something he wasn't ready for? I feel like I took his virginity and didn't even know." I blurt, the knot in my chest tightening with each word.

Olive leans back, studying me like she's trying to crack a code. "Gia, are you serious right now?"

"Yes!" I snap, throwing my hands in the air. "This is serious, Ols! What if I messed everything up for him?"

She leans forward, resting her elbows on her knees. "Okay, let's take a breath. First of all, I've known you my entire adult life, and if there's one thing I know, it's that you don't pressure people into anything. You're practically allergic to conflict."

"Not helping," I mutter.

"I'm serious," she continues. "Charlie's a grown-ass man. If he wasn't ready, he wouldn't have gone there. Period. Give him some credit, okay?"

Her words settle over me, soothing some of the guilt bubbling in my chest. "You really think so?"

"Absolutely. But... let's not ignore the real takeaway here."

"What's that?" I ask cautiously, narrowing my eyes.

She grins, the teasing light back in her gaze. "That after almost a decade of nothing, you're the one who made him break his streak—even if it was just a PG streak-breaking. If that's not game, I don't know what is."

"Oh my God," I groan, reaching for the pillow again to toss it at her.

The soft thud of fabric hitting her arm only makes her laugh harder, and despite myself, I feel a small smile tugging at my lips.

"Okay," I mutter, "can we just shut up about it and pick a film now, please?"

Olive leans back in her chair, her lips curling into that mischievous smile I know all too well. "Oh, I don't know, G. I was just getting started." She eyes me like a cat toying with its prey, and I immediately regret saying anything at all.

She scrolls through the streaming channels, her grin widening as her eyes dart over the options. "How about *The Forty-Year-Old Virgin*? Classic, right?" She nudges me with her elbow, and I feel my cheeks heat up.

I groan, dropping my head into my hands. "Olive... please, no."

But she's just warming up. "Ooh! Or what about *40 Days and 40 Nights*? You know, the one where he gives up sex for forty days. Sounds kinda... familiar, doesn't it?"

I stare at her, horrified. "You're actually going there?"

Olive shrugs, her expression all wide-eyed and innocent. "What? It's a classic. Besides, Josh Hartnett was practically a god in that movie. Or..." Her grin turns wicked. "We could get really educational and throw on *American Pie*. It does tackle virginity in a pretty... hands-on way."

I slap my hand to my forehead, groaning. "You're impossible. You know that, right?"

She laughs, grabbing a piece of sushi from the leftover spread on the coffee table. "Hey, I'm just curating a thematic experience. Virginity, celibacy, and baked goods—it's basically a commentary on life choices."

"Life choices," I snort, picking up a maki roll and popping it into my mouth. "I'm pretty sure no one wants their pies critiquing their decisions."

Olive waves a hand dismissively. "Hey, don't knock it till you try it. I mean, the pie didn't seem to mind."

"Oh my God, shut up," I mutter, scrolling through the options faster. "Can we please just pick something that doesn't involve virginity, celibacy, or baked goods?"

Olive shrugs, clearly pleased with herself. "Fine, fine. No virgin movies. I'll allow it."

I flick her arm, cracking a reluctant smile as the tension between us starts to ease. "Thank you. And know this... if you mention *40 Days and 40 Nights* again, I swear I'm blocking you on everything."

She gasps, clutching her chest like I've mortally wounded her. "Wow. The betrayal. But fine you pick."

I finally settle on *Pitch Perfect*, hitting play with a sigh of relief. "There. A movie with singing, bad jokes, and zero unnecessary discussions about pies."

Olive grins, stealing another piece of sushi. "Beca's eyeliner alone makes it a classic."

I laugh, leaning back into the couch as the opening scene plays, the scent of soy sauce and wasabi lingering in the air.

Olive tosses a pillow at me. "Don't get too emotional over there, songbird."

"I'm not," I lie, popping a maki roll into my mouth.

The aca-drama on screen is a welcome distraction, but underneath it, I feel that familiar tug. It's been years since I sang—*really* sang. Maybe it's just Charlie being here, stirring up all my nostalgic feels, but part of me still misses it. Even if I pretend I don't.

But for now, I focus on the movie and the leftover sushi, letting the beat of *"Don't Stop the Music"* drown out all the rest.

23

GIA

The Boy Who Blocked His Own Shot

My phone buzzes just as I'm queuing up the last post of the night, my brain foggy from sushi, sarcasm, and way too much second-hand singing. I glance at the screen and—yep. There it is. A single message, all casual like he doesn't know exactly what he's doing.

Charlie: How was movie night?

Gia: Barely survived

A smile tugs at my lips before I can stop it. I tell myself it's just the lingering high from bad puns and an over-the-top grand gesture. But it's also... him. Obviously.

Gia: NGL, I think Beca's eyeliner just triggered my emo core back into existence

Charlie: We both know it was never a phase ;)

I let out a quiet laugh, shaking my head like that'll stop the heat creeping up my neck. The screen lights up again before I've even thought of a comeback.

Charlie: What are you up to?

Gia: Scheduling some posts so Future Me doesn't have a breakdown tomorrow

Charlie: Sounds like you need a distraction...

Oh. *Okay.* A little thrill zips straight through me. Is he—? No. Wait. Is he flirting?

Gia: Are you actively trying to sabotage my career?

I chew on my lip as I hit send, already watching the screen with zero chill.

Charlie: Sabotage? Never. But I might be trying to steal a bit of your attention

Ugh. So smooth. Too smooth. I roll my eyes, even as I feel my entire face heating up like a teenager on MSN Messenger.

Gia: You might be succeeding. But don't get cocky

The typing bubble shows up instantly. Of course it does.

Charlie: Cocky? I was going for charming.
Clearly, I need to work harder

Gia: Clearly

There's a pause.

Charlie: So, what would it take to properly distract you? Hypothetically

It's silly late. I should shut this down, should close the app and get some sleep. But instead, my brain short-circuits, conjuring an image of him—shirtless, damp hair curling at the ends, smelling like that clean, warm soap that somehow lingers on his skin for hours.

My breath catches in my throat.

It's the way he says hypothetically. Like he's handing me the reins. Letting me set the pace. Letting me want him first.

I stare at the screen for a beat too long. Then I type, fingers moving before I can overthink it.

> Gia: Depends. How much effort are you willing to put in?

There's a pause—long enough for doubt to start creeping in. Maybe I pushed too far. Maybe I read him wrong.

Then—

> Charlie: If it's for you? As much as it takes

My stomach flips. The heat behind those words is undeniable, even through a screen. It's not just flirting anymore—it feels like *something*.

> Gia: Bold statement, Andersen. Prove it

No hesitation this time.

> Charlie: FaceTime me

My thumb hovers over the screen. My heart is thudding like a warning—or maybe a countdown. Nerves twist in my gut, tangled up with something that feels dangerously close to hope.

I don't even get the chance to decide.

The screen lights up. He's already calling.

I let out a quiet, nervous laugh before swiping to answer.

His face fills the screen, bathed in soft, golden light. His hair's tousled, like he's been dragging his hands through it—and now I kind of want to.

"Hey," he says, voice warm and low, the kind that wraps around you and settles deep.

"Hey yourself," I say, aiming for casual, but my voice comes out breathier than I'd like. My heart's doing Olympic-level gymnastics.

He studies me for a beat, his gaze flicking over my face.

"You look... focused," he says, mouth curving into the kind of smile that makes it very clear he knows exactly what he's doing.

"I was working, remember?" I tease, leaning back into the pillows like I'm not wildly aware of how I look through his screen. "But you, Chef, seem hell-bent on derailing my productivity."

"Guilty as charged." His grin spreads, slow and deliberate, and there's something in the way his gaze drags across the screen—like he's cataloguing every inch of me. "So... is it working?"

My breath catches.

There's nothing subtle about the way he's looking at me—like he's already got his hands on me in his head. I tug the blanket up over my chest, not to hide, just to do something with my hands. Suddenly, everything feels amplified. The soft lighting, the brush of cotton against skin, the heat pulsing at the base of my spine.

"That depends," I say, voice quieter now, the sass peeling back just a little. "What exactly are you trying to do, Charlie?"

He laughs—low, rough, the kind of sound that hits lower than it should.

"I don't know, G," he murmurs, and the way he says my name makes it feel like something intimate. "You tell me. What do you *think* I'm trying to do?"

The heat in his voice is unmistakable, and it sparks something inside me—a low, slow burn of thrill and temptation. I shift against the pillows, the blanket slipping slightly from my shoulder, revealing just a little more of the strap of my tank top.

His eyes follow the movement, and I catch the subtle flick of his throat as he swallows.

"I think you're trying to make me blush," I say, aiming for playful, though there's the faintest tremor threading through my voice.

His lips twitch into a smirk, but his gaze doesn't waver.

"Blush?" He leans in, his face filling more of the screen, voice lowering like it's meant for me alone. "Gia... I don't think you blush as easily as you want me to believe."

My heart thuds against my ribs as I tilt my head, feigning cool while everything inside me burns. "Oh, you think you know me that well?"

"Better than you think." His grin softens into something quieter. Something dangerous. "Let me prove it."

I arch a brow, pretending I'm still in charge here, even as my body betrays me. "And how exactly do you plan on doing that?"

His expression shifts—less teasing now, more intent. He angles the phone just enough to show skin; the smooth line of his bare chest, the curve of his shoulder, the sheet riding low across his hips. My breath catches.

"Let's just say I'm good at reading the room," he murmurs, voice a low rumble that thrums through my spine. "The question is, G... are you comfortable showing me what I've been thinking about all night?"

The heat in his words is bold, unapologetic—and it lights something wild in me. I hesitate for just a second, nerves colliding with want, and then slowly, deliberately, I let the blanket slip lower.

His eyes darken, his lips parting as he watches—silent, but so, so focused.

Charlie's gaze lingers, heavy and unblinking. His chest rises and falls in a measured rhythm, like he's reining himself in one breath at a time. "Careful, G," he murmurs, his voice low and laced with tension. "You're gonna make it really hard for me to behave."

The air shifts—thicker, hotter—and I don't even try to stop the words from spilling out. "Who says I want you to behave?"

The second I say it, heat floods my face, but it's too late. The thrill of it pulses through me like a live wire, my body answering a question I haven't said out loud yet.

His lips twitch, slow and deliberate, into a smile that could undo me all by itself. He shifts again, the phone tilting just enough to reveal another sliver of him—bare skin, lean muscle, and a shadow of ink that vanishes beneath the sheet at his waist.

"That's a dangerous thing to say to someone who's already struggling," he says, his voice rough around the edges now—like he's barely keeping it together.

I lean in, closer to the screen like I can actually close the distance between us. "Struggling with what?" I ask, my voice barely more than a breath.

His eyes don't leave mine. "With how much I want you right now."

The words hit like a spark in dry tinder—instant, electric. Every nerve in my body feels like it's lighting up from the inside.

I grip the edge of the blanket, knuckles white, fighting to keep my breathing even. "Then stop struggling," I whisper. "Show me."

For a moment, he doesn't move. His eyes search my face, his jaw tightening like he's holding back—like he's checking, really checking, that I mean it.

Then he moves.

He shifts the phone, propping it against something offscreen, freeing his hands. The angle changes, just slightly, and I get more of him now—his collarbone, the glint of sweat on his skin, the way the sheet clings low against his hips, barely holding on.

My pulse is thundering.

"Your turn, G," he says, voice like smoke and velvet, low and sure and utterly devastating.

My breath hitches, and I glance up at the screen, catching the steady weight of his gaze—waiting, patient, impossible to ignore.

Slowly, deliberately, I let the blanket slip away, leaving me bare to the thin straps of my tank top and the curve of my shoulders.

His eyes track every movement, sharp and hungry, and a wild surge of boldness rises inside me.

"Like this?" I ask, tilting my head just enough, letting my hair fall over one shoulder.

"Exactly like that," he replies, voice low, rough.

The air between us hums, thick and electric, even through the screen. He leans back just enough, and I get a full view of the lazy, confident way he sprawls against the pillows. His fingers trail along the edge of the sheet—slow, deliberate—like he's daring me to ask for more.

I can almost feel the heat radiating off him, smell the faint, musky scent that lingers beneath his skin.

"You're really going to make me work for this, aren't you?" I tease.

His grin deepens, eyes glittering with something sharp and hungry. "Only if you want me to."

I swallow hard, the weight of the moment pressing down like a physical force, heart pounding hard enough to echo in my ears. The screen feels like a lifeline between us, a silent dare hanging thick in the space.

"Show me," I breathe, voice low and steady. "Show me how you touch yourself."

Charlie's breath catches, sharp and audible, and for a long, suspended moment, he doesn't move. His eyes stay locked on me—searching, questioning—like he's trying to figure out if I really mean it.

"G," he murmurs, voice rough and uncertain, teetering on the edge of something fragile.

"Please," I whisper, the softness in my voice catching me off guard.

That's all it takes.

His hand dips lower, slipping just out of frame, and I watch, heart pounding, as his chest rises and falls with a ragged inhale.

He props the phone up against the headboard, angling it just right so I can see the lean lines of his torso, the sheet sliding further down—barely hiding the slow, deliberate beginnings of his movements.

My throat goes dry, and I can't tear my eyes away. Every movement he makes is slow, deliberate—like brushstrokes across skin, and I'm the only one watching the masterpiece unfold.

"Like this?" His voice is thick with desire, low and unsteady.

I nod, cheeks burning, warmth pooling deep in my belly. "Exactly like that," I whisper, mirroring his earlier words.

His gaze flickers back to the screen, lips curving into a wicked, sinful smile. "Your turn."

A rush of nerves flutters through my chest, but the way he's watching me—so intent, like I'm the only thing that exists—gives me the courage I need. Slowly, I let the blanket slip away, revealing myself in tiny gym shorts and a strappy crop top.

"Fuck, G. You're incredible, you know that?" His voice drops softer, reverent even, his movements never faltering.

The praise sends a jolt straight through me. I meet his gaze, hands trembling just enough as I adjust the camera. "Keep going," I murmur, feeling my confidence grow with every second.

"Only if you do," he counters, grin widening like he knows exactly how far this will go.

Okay. We're really doing this.

My pulse pounds loud in my ears as I dare myself to be bolder, to leave the past tangled up behind me.

The sheet slips lower, and my breath catches when his hand comes into view—fisting that thick, perfect cock. The swollen head glistens, slick with pre-cum under the dim light. My mouth waters. I want to taste him, take him deep, hear every sound he makes as he loses himself completely.

Heat pools low in my belly. I lick my lips, fingers sliding beneath the waistband of my shorts. I'm wet—so wet it's almost embarrassing—but the slick coating my fingers only pushes me further.

"Tell me how it feels, G," he murmurs, voice low and rough, all gravel and honey.

"It feels…" My breath shudders as my fingers find my clit, circling slow and deliberate, sending sparks shooting through me like live wires.

My eyes lock on the screen, on him, just as a bead of pre-cum trails down the length of his cock.

I lick my lips. God, I can't help myself.

"So good." My voice trembles—raw, needy. "Charlie, I'm so wet."

He sucks in a breath, loud and clear, his hand moving faster, firmer, syncing with the rhythm of my touch. The guttural groan that escapes him makes my stomach tighten, heat pooling even deeper.

"Yeah?" he rasps, voice thick with want. "Show me, G. Let me see how wet you are."

I hook my thumbs into the waistband of my shorts, sliding them down slow, my black lace thong sliding down with them. My pulse thunders in my ears as I tilt the phone, angling it just right.

The cool air from the fan brushes against my pussy, and a shiver snakes through me—half from nerves, half from something far hotter.

"Fuck, Gia." His voice drops low, almost guttural, rough with awe. "You're... so fucking beautiful."

His words hit me like a jolt of electricity. I bite my lip, the raw vulnerability hanging between us making everything pulse with tension.

"Touch yourself for me," he urges, his hand moving steadily over his cock. "I want to see exactly how good it feels."

I slide two fingers inside, breath hitching at the stretch as my body clenches around them. On the screen, Charlie lets out a low, guttural moan, his hand moving with an intensity that makes my pulse race.

"Charlie..." I moan, voice trembling with need.

His gaze burns through the screen, jaw clenched, fist gripping harder. "Show me," he demands, voice rough, thick with desire. "Show me your fingers. I want to see how wet you are for me."

I pull my fingers out, the sight almost too much—glistening strings of my arousal stretching between them, catching the light as I hold them up for him. My pussy throbs from the sudden emptiness.

"Fuck, Gia," he groans, head falling back as his hand speeds up, the wet, slick sounds of his strokes driving me wild. "You're perfect. So fucking perfect."

His voice is fire in my veins, heat pooling low and fierce. I shove my fingers back in, switching between desperate, rough circles on my clit and deep, greedy thrusts.

Charlie drives his hips into his palm, eyes squeezed shut, body trembling—and then he whimpers. Broken, needy—the sexiest sound I've ever heard.

I'm wound so tight, so close to the edge, that nothing could pull me out of this dizzying, feverish pull.

"Fuck." The word escapes him on a ragged breath as he watches me, those ocean eyes dark and heavy with lust, hooded and intense.

And it's my ultimate undoing.

I shatter under his gaze, my body bucking as I tumble over the edge, stars exploding behind my closed lids. Charlie's release follows, hips jerking, a string of incoherent words spilling from his perfect mouth, ribbons of cum splattering across the sheets.

I slump back, phone still in my palm, the weight of the moment pressing down as I watch him catch his breath. His eyes flutter open, a slow smile spreading across his face as reality settles back in.

For a beat, we just look at each other—room thick with the echo of what just happened. His chest rises and falls, eyes still heavy with heat.

My lips curve up, and we share a silent, knowing look that says everything without a word.

Then Charlie breaks the quiet, voice hoarse and warm. "You still there, G?"

I let out a shaky laugh, soft and uncertain. "Yeah, I'm here," I say, the simple words feeling fragile and real.

He shifts, leaning forward, a slow smirk tugging at the corner of his lips. "Good. 'Cause I'm not letting you go that easy."

A cold wave of dread crashes through me—part fear of losing him, part fear of letting him in. I'm caught between everything I want and everything I'm sure I can't have. I swallow hard, forcing myself to look away. "I should probably get some sleep."

His smile falters, the space between us tightening like a noose. I can see it in his eyes—unspoken, desperate. *Is that really what you want?* But instead of asking, he just nods, quiet. And the silence that settles afterward feels suffocating.

Charlie looks at me one last time, a softness in his eyes that nearly breaks me. Then, slow and gentle, he says, "Sleep well, G."

I nod, barely trusting my voice to answer, and watch as he hangs up—leaving a silence that feels impossibly loud.

My pulse hammers in my ears. This is my pattern—push away, build walls so thick even I can't find the cracks. But deep inside, I know it's not just the fear of him walking away again. It's that, even if he stays, a part of me will always be trapped—trapped in the past, tangled in the ache of a broken heart that still throbs with doubt, no matter how much I beg it to heal.

I want to let him in. I want to believe this is real—that he's here to stay, that we could be something more. But the part of me that clings to the past, to that old pain, won't let me. And I hate that I can't just be present, can't just be here with him. It's not fair—not to him, and not to me.

24

CHARLIE

You Be The Anchor That Keeps My Feet On The Ground, I'll Be The Wings That Keep Your Heart In The Clouds

Flour hangs in the air like smoke, settling on my skin, sticking to the sweat at my temples and the front of my shirt. I knead harder than I need to—palms digging into the dough, elbows tense, jaw clenched. My hands are red raw, but I don't stop. Won't stop. The rhythm is all I've got right now. If I pause for even a second, it all catches up with me.

It's been three hours since I hung up.

And I haven't sat down since.

Sleep isn't an option—not with her face still burned into the backs of my eyes. That look she had, like the weight of the past was dragging her under, and I was the one holding the rope. I keep replaying the way she laughed, the way we let go—just for a second. How easy it was. How fucking dangerous.

I shouldn't be thinking about the way she sounded when she came. Or how she looked at me after, like she almost wanted to believe this could be something real. I could've told her everything then. That I never stopped. That it's always been her.

But something in her changed—shut down—before the words had the chance to make it out. One blink and she was gone again. Walled off. Like I imagined the whole thing.

So now I'm here. Making cardamom dough at three in the morning. Trying not to drown in it.

The dough turns sticky, rough—overworked. I've gone too hard at it, but I knew that before I started. Wasn't really trying to make anything anyway. Just needed something to do with my hands. Something to stop me thinking.

I scrape it off the counter with a muttered curse and dump it straight into the bin. It lands with a heavy, wet thud. Pathetic. Hours wasted trying to find some kind of order in the mess. Trying to hold on to something I already feel slipping.

I clean up fast, scrubbing the counters until they shine, like that's going to help. Flour under my nails, sweat sticking to the back of my neck. My arms are burning. Doesn't matter. I'll take the ache over the silence.

It's the quiet that kills me—makes it impossible to shut her out. Gia, with that look in her eyes like she wanted to trust me. Like she almost did.

But she didn't.

Not yet.

I flip off the kitchen light and stand there in the dark. The silence presses in, thick and suffocating. My pulse pounds in my ears. I'm about to drag myself to bed when something catches—just the faintest flicker.

A torch.

Outside.

The beam cuts across the yard, erratic. Sharp bursts of light. Shadows twitch and stretch in every direction. My first thought is fox. Maybe a cat. But my gut's already saying something else.

Someone.

Then the porch light flicks on, soft and sudden, and the whole thing feels unreal. Like I've stepped out of time.

I don't stop to think. I just open the door.

The air hits cool and damp. My feet hit the porch steps before I even register the movement. And there she is.

Gia.

Standing in the half-light like she doesn't know how she got here. Hair a mess, eyes wide.

"Gia?" Her name leaves my mouth like a breath I've been holding. Like I'm scared she'll disappear if I say it too loud.

Her eyes find mine, and for a second I don't trust what I'm seeing. She looks almost ethereal—like something pulled from a dream I've had too many times. Or not enough. Hair tousled, eyes glassy, like she ran here straight from sleep and couldn't stop herself.

"I can't sleep," she says, voice thin and frayed at the edges.

Something tightens in my chest, sharp and sudden. I don't know if it's relief or panic. Maybe both. Maybe

I've finally tipped over the edge, conjuring her up out of nothing because I need her that badly.

I swallow hard.

"You're not a dream, are you?" It comes out quieter than I meant it to. A bad joke wrapped around something real. Too real.

Gia steps forward, eyes locked on mine, and something in me just... gives. I don't care if this is real or if my brain's cracked under the weight of wanting her. She's here. That's all I need.

Her hands press to my chest—warm, unsteady. My breath catches.

She rises onto her toes, and her lips brush mine. Barely there. Just a whisper. But it's enough to wreck me. My heart stutters, reaching for more, greedy for it.

For a second, everything goes quiet. The cool air. The world. It all fades out. There's just her—soft mint on her mouth, the heat rolling off her skin, the space between us shrinking to nothing.

She pulls back, just enough to look at me. Her eyes search mine, wide and unsure. And I know—I'm not the only one spinning.

"Charlie," she breathes. Barely a sound. But it undoes me.

"Come here." It comes out rough.

Then I'm kissing her. No hesitation, no space between us. Just need.

It's messy, urgent—her mouth against mine, our bodies flush, like she's always meant to fit there. I hold her tighter. Letting go isn't an option. Not anymore.

And for the first time in too long, I let myself feel it. All of it.

She's here.

I'm not dreaming.

She's it. The thing I didn't know I was missing until she showed up and knocked the wind out of me. The reason everything else has felt off.

She's everything. Always has been.

Her lips leave mine, and she rests her forehead against my chin. I breathe her in—vanilla and something warm. Familiar. She smells like home. Like summer clinging to my skin long after the sun's gone down.

And I feel it—how close we are. To something real. Something that could break just as easily as it builds.

The silence isn't heavy anymore. It's thick with everything we haven't said. Everything we're still scared to.

"G?"

"Don't." Her voice is quiet but sharp, her eyes locking on mine, steady. Pulling me back down to earth.

I nod, though I'm not even sure what I was asking.

She's captivating like this—bare-faced, honest, beautiful in a way that makes it hard to breathe.

"Don't be gentle with me, Charlie. But don't break me again. I'm not sure I could handle it."

Her words hit me like a gut punch. The kind you see coming but can't dodge.

The air thickens, cool against my skin but hot in my chest. She's handing me everything, and all I can think about is how easy it would be to screw it up.

My mouth opens—nothing comes out.

And then she kisses me.

Harder, deeper. No room for hesitation.

This time, I don't hold back. Not even a little.

Her hands skim up my chest, nails catching just enough to make me shiver. Then her palms flatten, pushing me inside. The door slams shut behind us, loud and final, but I barely hear it over the rush in my ears.

We crash into each other like we've been starved. Hands, mouths, teeth—no rhythm, no plan. Just need.

I kiss her like I've been dead and she's the only thing that ever made me feel alive.

I press her to the wall, lips back on hers before I can think. She gasps into my mouth, and I drink it in. Her fingers yank at the hem of my shirt—impatient. I pull it over my head and let it fall.

She's on me the second it's gone—hot, open-mouthed kisses dragging across my collarbone, my throat, teeth catching at my shoulder like she's trying to mark me.

"Gia," I groan, grabbing her hips, pulling her in like I could fuse us together if I tried hard enough.

She tilts her head back, eyes blown wide and wild.

And fuck—she's never looked more beautiful.

"Don't stop," she whispers, voice shaking. Her fingers are already at my waistband, tugging it loose with urgency.

I spin us, lift her just enough to set her on the edge of the counter. Her legs hook around my waist, pulling me in tight. I press into her, hands shoving under her tank top, rough and greedy. I need skin. I need her.

She gasps when I touch her, and that's all it takes—I yank the top off, drop it. She's bare now. Flushed. Perfect.

My mouth finds her breast, sucking hard, while my fingers roll and tease the other, watching her come undone against the cabinets. She arches into me like she's daring me to lose control.

She slides out of her leggings, and all that's left is a black lace thong that makes me forget how to breathe.

Her hands trail down my stomach, slow and certain, fingertips skimming the waistband of my shorts. She hooks a finger in the drawstring and gives it a playful tug before loosening the knot. When she pushes them down over my hips, that's it—I'm gone.

I kick them off in a rush, and then we're bare. Skin to skin. Nothing between us.

I kiss her like I need it to breathe—deep, hard, desperate. Like maybe this is how I make up for all the times I fucked it up.

"Charlie," she gasps, voice breaking as her fingers twist into my hair.

I press my forehead to hers, hands framing her face, thumbs stroking her cheeks.

"Are you sure?" she asks.

Her voice is soft, but the weight of it hits me hard.

My chest goes tight, but the answer's already there, sitting on my tongue.

"I've never been more sure of anything in my life."

She smiles—a soft curve of her lips—and it knocks the air right out of me. "I was hoping you'd say that," she whispers, her hands sliding down my back, holding on like she's scared I might vanish.

I lift her without thinking, carrying her through the kitchen and down the hall. Our mouths don't part for a second. By the time we hit the bedroom, we're both shaking—breathless, strung so tight it hurts.

I lay her down slow, careful, even though my whole body's screaming to have her. I hover over her, kiss her skin, her collarbone, her breasts, the dip of her waist. I tease just below her belly button, and she arches up with a gasp, clutching at my shoulders.

She's restless under me, her body already begging for more.

Mine is too. But I'm not rushing this. I can't.

I kiss my way back up, dragging my mouth along her throat, her chest, the hollow just below her neck. I take in every sound she makes, every shift of her hips. I want to remember all of it.

My hand slides between her thighs, slow. She gasps, her breath catching as I press against her, and fuck—

That sound? It undoes me.

"You're so fucking wet," I breathe, the words slipping out before I can stop them.

She's warm and open beneath me, slick and ready, and it hits me all at once—how badly I want to be inside her, how badly I want this to mean something.

Her legs tighten around my waist, pulling me in. "Please, Charlie," she whimpers, voice cracking. "I need you."

Fuck. My cock throbs at the sound of it, leaking already.

I pull back just enough to stand, chest heaving. My briefs come off in one rough motion, kicked somewhere behind me. I'm trembling with it now—every muscle tight, strung out.

I look down at her, and she looks right back—eyes dark, full of heat, full of want. Wild and wrecked and right here.

Mine.

Gia slides her thong down slowly, the lace catching on her thighs before pooling at her feet. She shifts, getting comfortable—but her eyes never leave mine.

"How do you want me?" she asks, breathless. There's a challenge in her voice. A plea, too.

"I want you in every way, Gia. Heart, mind body, soul." My voice is hoarse, raw with the weight of it. I crawl over her, caging her in, our faces barely apart. My nose brushes hers. "But right now... I need to see your face when you come."

Her breath stutters, her lips part. She doesn't answer—she doesn't need to. Her hips lift, subtle but certain, guiding me in.

I slide my cock between her thighs, groaning at the feel of her heat—slick and perfect. She trembles under me, her whole body arching as I press in. Her nails bite into my shoulders when the head of my cock pushes past her entrance.

"Fuck. Gia," I choke out, inch by inch sinking into her, feeling her stretch around me.

She's so fucking tight. So warm. So right.

And I don't ever want to let her go.

"Fuck, you feel amazing." My heart's pounding—like it's trying to rip right out of my chest. Every nerve's on fire. I want her. Need her. More than anything, ever.

I slow, just for a second, letting the tension hang between us. The air is thick, heavy. Her eyes lock on mine—wild, breath shallow—and I'm lost in her. Her beauty. Her fire. Her heat.

"That's it, Charlie. Right there," she breathes, voice trembling. She pulls me closer, hands digging into my shoulders, body pressing hard against mine rocking with me. "Fuck. I knew you'd feel this good."

Her words send my mind spiralling. Thank God I got off a few hours ago—otherwise, I'd be breaking world records. She deserves a marathon, not a sprint.

We both do.

I steady myself, one hand pressed into the mattress, the other gripping her ass, pulling her tight until there's no space left between us. Her fingers rake down my back, sharp and frantic, sending electric jolts through me. We're desperate—like no matter how close we get, it's not enough.

She's panting beneath me, breath ragged, every shuddering gasp pushing me deeper, harder.

"Charlie... please... more," she gasps, her legs locking tighter around me.

I can feel her—all of her—and it still isn't enough.

My hips slam into hers, skin slapping skin, the sound raw and filthy, mingling with her moans.

"Fuck, Gia... you feel unreal. Keep squeezing me like that." I'm barely breathing, words thick and ragged as control slips away.

Her nails dig into my back, her moans rising—raw, desperate. "Fuck... I'm so close..."

I want to hold on, to stretch this out, make it last. But my body's a traitor—pressure building, throbbing so fucking hard I don't know how much longer I can hold it.

My cock's straining, desperate for release, but I force myself to slow, gripping her hips tighter, trying to hold onto something—anything.

"Please, Charlie... don't stop," she breathes, nails digging into my back, pulling me closer as she arches into me, hungry for more.

I let out a rough breath, trying to stave off the inevitable, but fuck, she feels too good. I want this slow, sweet—but the need to finish is brutal.

My hands drop to her breasts, squeezing hard, lips crashing down to suck a hardened nipple into my mouth.

She moans—soft, desperate—and her fingers tangle in my hair, pulling me deeper. "Fuck, Charlie, just like that," she gasps, voice thick, breath ragged, hips grinding against me like she's trying to merge into my skin. "Your mouth... it's... oh my God."

I suck one nipple hard, fingers teasing the other, and she lets out a moan that slams into my chest, making my pulse spike.

Her whole body's trembling, and the way she calls my name—how her legs clamp down tight—it's pushing me over the edge.

"Kiss me, Charlie." Her whisper pulls me down, tongues tangling, heat sparking between us like wildfire. That's it—the dam breaks.

I lose it, pouring myself into her, every bit of me crashing deep inside. Her muscles clench around me, moans muffled against my mouth, and I bury my face in the curve of her neck, trying to catch my breath.

I hold her close, too wired to pull away, heart beating like a goddamn drum, both of us drenched in the aftermath—the soft rise and fall of her breath, the warmth of her skin pressed against mine.

For a moment, it's just us—raw, tangled, and exactly where we need to be.

Her laughter bubbles up from deep inside her, warm and light, catching me completely off guard. I freeze for a second, still buried inside her, heart hammering in my chest.

She pulls back just enough to lock eyes with me, a glint of mischief shining in her gaze.

"What's so funny, Perelli?" I ask, breathless, trying to catch up with the storm of feelings swirling inside me.

She grins—playful, wicked—and then can't hold it in anymore. She bursts into laughter again, the sweetest, most genuine sound I've ever heard.

"I can't believe I just popped your cherry," she teases, voice full of affection beneath the playfulness.

I shake my head, laughing too, disbelief and warmth flooding through me. "You didn't really—but okay, let's go with that."

The weight of what just happened settles over me, heavy and real, like a blanket I never want to let go of.

She leans up, lips soft and teasing against mine, then pulls back just enough to whisper, "Well, you sure looked like a man who hadn't been laid in a while."

Before I can even respond, she giggles, the sound filling the space between us—light, effortless, and somehow grounding.

I take a slow, deep breath, my chest tight with something I can't quite name. The moment is perfect, and yet beneath it all, there's an ache I can't shake.

"I'm glad it was you," I say quietly, voice rough with everything I feel but can't say.

"Me too," she replies, a small, genuine smile curving her lips.

The silence that follows is heavy, hanging between us like a whispered confession. Words press on my tongue, but I can't find them. So I start to pull away, moving to create distance from the vulnerability tangled inside me.

But then she stops me, her hand resting gently but firmly on my chest.

"Wait," she says, her voice small and tentative, like she's unsure if she should even ask. Her eyes flick up to meet mine, soft but searching.

"I know this is a UTI waiting to happen," she says, voice low. "But I just... want to fall asleep like this. With you inside me."

My heart skips a beat. I freeze for a moment, caught off guard by the vulnerability in her request. And yet something about it makes me melt all over again.

"Yeah," I murmur, nodding, my hand lifting to trace the curve of her cheek softly. "Yeah, sure."

We settle into the quiet, her body pressing close, and I stay inside her. Anchored. Moored. Grounded.

The room feels peaceful now, heavy with the weight of unspoken promises and everything we are—lingering in the stillness until sleep finally claims us.

25

GIA

Dark Blue

This is self-sabotage at its finest. But damn, does it feel good.

Charlie's asleep in the other room while I sit at his kitchen table, staring into my black coffee, stewing over everything that's been fucking with my head these past few weeks.

How everything somehow fell into place. How I just... forgave him.

The old me would never.

But I'm starting to like this softer, more forgiving version of myself. Patient. Quiet in a way that feels strange but not unwelcome. I could get used to her—even if she still feels a little foreign.

I scroll idly through my inbox, barely paying attention—until a subject line jumps out and slaps me in the face.

From: marketing@lustrecollection.com
Subject: Exclusive Partnership Opportunity — Lustre Collection Hotels

My heart skips. The Lustre Collection? The boutique hotel chain that's basically an Instagrammers paradise?

I open the email, my eyes racing over the first few lines:

Dear Ms Perelli,

We've been following your work and would love to discuss an exclusive collaboration opportunity. As the flagship property of the Lustre Collection, Paloma Bay has been a longtime admirer of your aesthetic and brand. With our upcoming launch of several new properties across Europe, we are seeking an official influencer and ambassador to represent Lustre Collection Hotels over the next year, starting with our newest addition; the Malfi Luxe in Rome, Italy.

This would include:

– Exclusive stays at our flagship and newly launched properties.

– Collaborative content creation campaigns.

– A generous financial package and additional perks.

We would love to discuss this opportunity further and provide more details.

Looking forward to hearing from you.

Best regards,

The Lustre Collection Team

Holy shit. My pulse races as I read it again. They're not just offering me a stay; they're talking about a year-long contract to represent their brand across Europe. They're launching new properties, and they want me to be the face of it.

Me.

Immediately, I grab my phone and call Olive.

"Hey, what's up?" She sounds like she's just woken up, or maybe she's just groggy from a lack of caffeine.

"I need you to pinch me," I blurt out.

"Uh, why?" she says, the sleepiness quickly giving way to curiosity.

"I just got an email. From the Lustre Collection. They want me to be their content creator—like, *the* content creator—for a year. Ibiza, Italy, the works." My words tumble out in a rush, my heart still pounding.

There's a pause. "Wait—what?" Olive's voice goes up an octave, fully awake now. "You mean the Lustre Collection? As in... Paloma Bay?"

"Yes!"

"Holy shit, G!" She practically squeals. "This is massive! What did you say?"

"I literally just opened the email," I admit, pacing the kitchen. "I needed someone to freak out with first."

"Well, you called the right person. Freaking out is my specialty," she says. I can practically hear her grinning. "So, what's the next step? Are you saying yes?"

"Yes? Maybe? I don't know. This feels... huge, Ols. What if I screw it up? What if it's a scam?"

"Gia, listen to me," she says, her tone turning serious. "You've worked your ass off for an opportunity like this.

They wouldn't reach out if they didn't believe in you. Now, take a deep breath, reply to that email, and make it happen. You've got this."

Her words hit me like a shot of caffeine. She's right. I've been dreaming of something like this for years, and now that it's here, I can't let doubt get in the way.

There's just one thing. One person. One maddening complication putting doubts in my head.

And he's just walked in, looking like a fucking god.

Hair rumpled, sweatpants slung low on his hips, bare chest catching the morning light like it's a goddamn spotlight. It's criminal how he makes looking good so effortless.

My pulse stutters. Damn him. Damn him for making this complicated.

"Gia?" Olive's voice snaps me out of my trance.

"Uh, I've gotta go, I'll take to you later," I mumble, barely registering her goodbye before I hang up.

Charlie leans against the doorway, a lazy, almost smug smile tugging at the corner of his lips. "Morning."

My heart's doing cartwheels, and I hate it. Or maybe I don't. Either way, the timing couldn't be worse.

My mind races, a thousand scenarios running in parallel like a high-speed chase. What if it's a scam? Maybe I should email back right now and see if it's legit... but what if it's all too good to be true? A year-long contract with the Lustre Collection, representing hotels across Europe? It's everything I've ever dreamed of.

But what if I'm just jumping the gun? Maybe it's better to play it cool, think it through. A discussion won't hurt, right? It's a once-in-a-lifetime opportunity... but still.

I glance at Charlie, his casual stance only adding to the weight of everything I'm thinking. Should I tell him?

No. Not now. I don't want to ruin the moment, not when everything feels so... easy. So right.

I need to sort my head out first.

Charlie clears his throat, breaking through the haze of my thoughts. "You want breakfast?"

"Uh, no, I'm okay, thanks."

Charlie's brow furrows in confusion, his eyes narrowing just slightly. "What's up?" he asks, voice softer now.

"Nothing," I say, trying my best to hide whatever's written all over my face. I'm not sure I'm succeeding.

But he's already moving toward me, his every step pulling my attention like gravity. The way he pushes off the doorframe, his body moving with that effortless confidence, does things between my legs that I really don't have time for.

Now is not the moment to be getting distracted.

"Come on, you're the worst liar in the world," he says, smirking as he steps closer. "I know when something's up."

I say nothing, my eyes pleading with him to drop it.

"Okay. Your call," he shrugs, bypassing me to pour himself a coffee.

Why? Why can't I keep this from him? Why does it feel like I owe him the truth, after he just up and left without me?

I follow him into the kitchen, the need to be honest pushing through the petty frustration.

"I got an email," I say, my voice tight. "From the Lustre Collection. It's a group of retro boutique hotels in Europe."

"And?" he presses.

"And they want to talk about collaborating."

"So that's what the screaming was about." He smirks, sipping his coffee. "Sounds fucking awesome, G." He pauses for a beat, his eyes flicking over me before he adds, "So what's the issue?"

"Not an issue, per se, but it's a year-long contract."

The silence stretches between us. I want to say more, but the words feel tangled in my throat.

"Obviously, I don't want to assume this means anything," I say, voice catching slightly as I gesture between us. "I know you're going back to Aus eventually, and—"

He cuts me off, voice low and rough. "You don't want to assume?"

Heat pulses in his gaze as he sets his coffee down with a soft clink. He turns, blue eyes piercing mine. "Let me stop you right there, G. This means everything. You're everything. There, I said it. After twelve fucking years."

He runs a hand through his hair, frustration and something deeper shaking his voice. "Do you have any idea what it's been like? Seeing you again pretending I don't want..." He falters, eyes dropping to the floor, then back to me—soft, burning. "Knowing you hated me. Probably cursed my name every time you thought of me. That was the hardest part. Because I deserved it. But it killed me."

My throat tightens, heart twisting.

"Your happiness, G..." He sighs, shaking his head, searching for words. "It's everything to me. I don't give a shit if I have to—"

His voice cracks, and I can't let him finish.

I grab the back of his neck, pull him close, and crash my lips to his.

He moans against my mouth, needy and raw, and it sends heat pooling between my legs. My breath hitches, heart pounding in my chest, as his fingers tangle in my hair, tugging at my scalp just enough to make me gasp.

He pulls me closer, as if there's no space left to breathe, the edges of our bodies blurring until we're no longer two separate people, just one. It's just him. Just us. Nothing else exists. Not that it ever did.

I spent years convincing myself I hated him, but deep down, I never stopped loving him.

It's always been him.

"G," he breathes, his voice strained with hunger. He presses against me, his arousal unmistakable, as his hands slide under me. Before I can even process, he lifts me effortlessly onto the kitchen island. The cool surface bites against my bare thighs, a sharp contrast to the fire consuming me.

His mouth crashes against mine again, stealing my breath, making my knees weak. His warm, calloused hands grip my thighs, prying them apart as he slots himself between them.

"I'm not going anywhere, G. I'm not leaving you again."

The words slam into me, rattling something loose in my chest. Is this just heat-of-the-moment, or does he really mean it? But all my thoughts turn to the way his fingers skim higher, teasing, torturing, making my body beg for it, for him.

"Fuck, I want you so much," he rasps, yanking at the waistband of my shorts. His hand slides inside, cupping my pussy through the damp lace of my thong. I gasp, tilting my hips into his touch, desperate for more.

My fingers tangle in his hair, pulling him back in, kissing him harder. Deeper. The heat coiling low in my belly is relentless, impossible to ignore. I never want to stop kissing him.

He pushes the lace aside, and my breath hitches as he slides a finger along my slit.

"I love how wet you are for me," he rasps, his breath hot against my mouth as he pushes a thick finger inside me.

"So ready. So tight. So perfect."

"Charlie—"

Fuck.

I don't get to finish. Words crumble into nothing when he slides in another finger, stretching me, stealing my breath, leaving me gasping.

He doesn't hesitate, doesn't let up. My body clenches around his fingers—desperate, aching for more. My pussy throbs when he withdraws, spreading my arousal over my clit, circling, teasing, bringing me closer to the edge.

"Fuck, Charlie. You're going to make me come," I say, breathless.

"That's the fucking point." His smile is sinful, addictive, enough to melt the panties off a nun.

He kisses me again, hard and desperate, claiming me with a hunger that leaves me breathless, pressing on my clit before withdrawing his hands completely from my underwear.

"Lay down. Let me look at you," he says.

I do as he says, my breath shallow as I shift back onto the counter, slipping out of my shorts and thong in a single, fluid motion.

Charlie's eyes darken as he watches, his tongue swiping across his bottom lip. Then he shoves his sweatpants and boxers down in one swift move, his cock springing free—thick, heavy, and veined, a bead of precum glistening on the tip.

Without hesitation, he positions himself between my legs, gripping my thighs as he sinks into me, stretching, filling me. I revel in the feeling—the closeness, the connection—it's everything.

His hands hook beneath my legs, lifting them over his thick forearms as he drives into me, gripping my hips, pressing me into the hard surface of the island. It'll probably leave bruises, but I don't care—not when he feels this good.

I gasp, fingers curling around the edge of the counter, my spine arching as he slams into me, fucking me like he can't get enough, like he's making up for lost time.

"I fucking missed you, Gia," he rasps, his voice rough, low, and thick with need.

I can barely catch my breath, but the words spill out anyway, raw and unfiltered. "I missed you too."

"Fuck. I can't get enough of you." He goes harder, deeper, punching the air from my lungs with every raw, relentless thrust, as if hearing my truth has unlocked some insatiable, primal need to be closer than close—souls touching, bodies fused. He's so fucking deep I feel it in my stomach, a sharp, pleasure-laced ache that reminds me he's here. He's real.

It feels like the years apart never really existed. Like all my hatred, all my broken parts, are being slowly pieced back together by the one person who shattered them in the first place. It's bittersweet, the way he makes my chest ache.

"Yes, G, just like that. Fuck, you're taking me so well," Charlie rasps, his voice rough and wrecked.

Strung tight, my body trembles, every nerve ending alight as I teeter on the edge. His hand slides between us, fingers finding my clit with infuriating precision—circling, pressing, flicking—the perfect pressure sending shockwaves through me, straight to my core.

"Fuck, Charlie," I gasp, my voice hoarse, raw.

"That's it, G. Come for me," he growls, his thrusts relentless, his fingers ruthless.

And I do. I shatter around him, my pussy clenching, desperate and greedy, pulling him deeper as the world blurs, the edges dissolving into nothing but him.

My orgasm crashes through me, sharp and blinding, a pulsing that starts deep, stealing my breath and my heart as it ripples out, leaving me trembling. Raw. Undone.

And so incredibly vulnerable.

His grip tightens on my hips, fingers digging in as his thrusts turn quick and shallow, his legs trembling as he drives into me.

"Fuck, Gia," he groans, voice wrecked, weak with need. Dirty blonde hair slicks his forehead, mouth open, breath hot and ragged. His hips jerk once, twice—then he's spilling inside me, warmth flooding, his body tense, shaking.

I watch him, savouring every second of his release. He's achingly beautiful when he comes, every inch of him consumed by pleasure, his face a perfect mix of raw need and satisfaction. He stays there, buried deep, his hands gripping my hips like he's afraid to let go—like if he does, this moment might disappear. Like I might disappear.

I stay perfectly still, feeling the warmth of him inside me, the weight of his body pressing me into the counter, anchoring me to the moment. To him. My breath slows, steady but uneven at the edges, the silence thick with something raw and uncertain.

Suspended in the afterglow, we linger, until slowly, he retreats. Instinctively, my body shivers at the loss of him. Emptiness creeps in, sharp and sudden, but before it can settle, I push up on my elbows, reaching for him. He's already there, meeting me halfway, his lips finding mine in a kiss that starts soft—a promise, a plea, a prayer. But it builds, growing hungry, desperate, caught in an endless loop of want and need.

He slides his arms beneath me, and I hook mine around his neck, wrapping my legs around his waist as he lifts me effortlessly, carrying me to the sofa.

He lowers me gently, like I'm something fragile, but the second I'm down, he follows, his weight a comforting press against me. His mouth finds mine again—soft at first, like he's savouring me, like he's memorising the shape of my lips. But then it shifts, hunger seeping in, his kiss deepening, growing desperate, like he can't get enough, like he's afraid I'll disappear if he stops.

His hands roam—gripping my thighs, sliding up my sides, tangling in my hair—pulling me closer even though there's no space left between us. I can taste the need on his tongue, feel it in the way his hips start to grind against me, lazy but purposeful, like his body's moving on instinct, already craving more.

"I don't ever want to stop kissing you," he rasps against my mouth, his breath hot, voice wrecked.

"Then don't," I whisper, my fingers threading through his hair, pulling him back to me.

We keep going—kissing until our breaths are ragged, until his cock stirs against me, hardening with every roll of his hips, every desperate sound caught between us. His hand slips between my thighs, his fingers teasing, but it's not enough. I need more.

"Use me, G," he murmurs, his voice a low growl against my skin. "Fuck, I want you to use my cock."

Heat floods me, sharp and instant, my body aching with the same need he's spilling into every word.

"Talk dirty to me," I breathe, my voice trembling, not from fear but from how badly I want him—every filthy word, every raw, wrecked sound.

His lips curve into a dark smile against my neck, and then he does—his words as sinful as the way he touches me.

His lips trail from my mouth to my jaw, then down my neck, leaving a path of heat in their wake. His voice is low, rough against my skin.

"You feel so fucking good, G. I could spend forever buried in you, just like this."

His hand slides down my body, fingers brushing over sensitive skin, making me shiver.

"I love the way you fall apart for me. The way your pussy clenches like it doesn't want to let me go."

He shifts slightly, grinding against me, already growing hard again, his breath ragged.

"You want me hard again, don't you? Want to ride my cock, use me to make yourself come?"

His fingers tease between my legs, just light enough to make me whimper.

"Tell me how bad you want it, G. Tell me you need me."

"I do. I fucking need you." My voice is raw, desperate, pathetic.

"Fuck, yeah. That's it. Show me how greedy you are for my cock. Take what you need."

His lips hover over mine, his breath hot, teasing. His fingers slide lower, barely brushing where I need him most.

"Look at you," he rasps, his voice a gravelly whisper. "So fucking wet for me. You like this, don't you? Being so full of me you can't even think straight."

I arch into him, desperate, and he grins, wicked and soft all at once.

"You're fucking addicted, G. Just like I am. Can't get enough of you—your taste, those addictive little noises you make, the way you squeeze my cock with your perfect little cunt. It's like you were made for me."

His hand slides to my throat, not squeezing, just resting there, his thumb stroking lazily against my pulse.

"I want to hear you beg for it. Tell me how bad you need me inside you again."

"Fuck. Please, Charlie."

"Harder," he tsks.

Defiance has me in a chokehold. I hate sounding so needy, so desperate. But the ache between my legs betrays me. "I need you. I need you so bad it hurts." When he doesn't say anything, I continue. "Fuck me again, Charlie. Again and a-fucking-gain. Make a mess of me. I'm yours."

His growl vibrates against my skin. "Good girl. That's it. You're all mine. Fucking take me. Use me, G. Make yourself come on my cock, ruin me for anyone else—like you haven't already."

His hips grind into mine, growing harder with every word, his mouth trailing down to my chest, biting, sucking, leaving marks, claiming me.

"You drive me fucking insane. Look at you—so desperate, so beautiful when you're falling apart for me. Come sit on my lap, baby. Fuck that pretty little cunt on me until you come."

His words send me completely feral, untethered, like he's reached inside me and pulled at something primal.

I sit up, pushing him back, straddling him with a hunger that feels stitched into my skin. My hair falls around us like a veil, turning the world into just him and me. It's a struggle to keep my mouth away from his, like we're magnets straining against invisible forces.

I grind down, chasing the friction, the throb of his arousal hot and insistent against me. The ache sharpens, unbearable. I can't take it anymore.

I lower myself onto him, gasping at the stretch, the way he fills me, claiming every inch like he belongs there. And maybe he does. Maybe he always did.

I roll my hips, slow and deliberate, controlling every delicious thrust. His hands find my hips, fingers digging in like he's afraid I'll slip away. His mouth is everywhere—on mine, my neck, my nipples—leaving trails of heat that spark beneath my skin.

He feels like home—not the safe, quiet kind, but the kind that lives in your bones, stitched into the fabric of who you are. Familiar, grounding. The place you come back to even when you don't mean to.

But he's excitement too—wild, electric, like standing at the edge of something dangerous and not giving a fuck if you fall.

And maybe that's what this is. Falling. Fast and hard. And not wanting to stop.

Did I ever stop falling? Even when I hated him? Even when we were strangers?

Maybe I've been falling this whole time, crashing through every version of myself, every version of him, and I'm only just now hitting the ground.

And it feels like heaven. Like hell. Like both, tangled so tight I can't tell where one ends and the other begins.

I rock my hips harder, like I'm angry at myself for wanting him this much, for needing him in ways I can't control. For the inevitable future—the part where this burns out, crashes, leaves me hollow. But I can't stop. I don't want to stop.

Because right now, he's mine. Right now, I can pretend this doesn't end.

"You're being such a good boy for me," I gasp out, the words slipping free before I even register them.

Silence.

For a beat, everything stills—my breath, his movements. The words hang between us, heavy and unexpected. My eyes widen slightly, heat flooding my face.

Shit. Did I really just say that?

But then—

Charlie's grip tightens. His jaw clenches. And his eyes—fuck—they darken, pupils blown wide with something feral, something hungry.

"Say that again," he rasps, voice wrecked, hips bucking up hard, deeper, like he's trying to fuck the words right back out of me.

My breath stutters, but there's no going back now. I lean in, lips brushing his ear, voice low and smug even though my heart's racing.

"You're being such a good boy for me."

The groan that rips from his throat is pure filth, primal and desperate. He flips us without warning, pinning me beneath him, his face inches from mine, breath hot, wild.

"You think you can handle me being your good boy, G?" he growls, thrusting hard enough to knock the air from my lungs. "'Cause I'll be whatever you want—as long as you keep saying shit like that."

I gasp, nails digging into his back, head tipping back with a sharp, breathless laugh.

"Then be good and make me come."

His grin is wicked, all teeth and sin. "Yes, boss," he says.

And he does.

26

GIA

A Decade Under the Influence

I'm soup. Like someone tossed me into a pot and stirred me around a few times. All limp and warm and just... here.

And... did I just say limp? Ugh, gross, Gia. Get it together.

The only thing about the last night that isn't limp? Charlie's ridiculous manhood.

Oh god, I just said *manhood*.

I'm officially a walking cringe factory.

I'm blaming lack of sleep and being fucked delirious by the man I've hated half my life.

I should be over the moon, but I just feel a little... empty.

The Lustre Collection is a huge deal. A break in my career is all I ever wanted. But now that Charlie's here—and staying—I'm confused as hell. The last thing I want is for my feelings to eclipse everything I've spent working towards my entire life.

I glance over at Charlie, my thoughts too loud to let me sleep. He's out cold, his breathing slow and steady, the kind of deep sleep that comes easy to people who don't overthink everything. His face looks softer like this, all the sharp edges smoothed out, the weight he carries nowhere to be seen. His unfairly long lashes cast shadows against his cheekbones, and his lips are slightly parted, the rise and fall of his chest hypnotic.

My eyes trace the lines of him—the way the sheet sits low on his hips, the tattooed arm stretched above his head, the mess of dirty blonde hair that's always just a little unruly. Even in sleep, there's a faint crease between his brows, like his dreams might be giving him something to think about.

I turn onto my side, watching him, because it's too easy to look. Too easy to want to reach out, to press my fingers to the rough stubble on his jaw just to feel the warmth of him. But I don't. Instead, I stay still, my mind tangled between what I want and what I should do. My career on one side of the scale, this—whatever this is—tipping the other.

Then Charlie shifts, turning slightly toward me, murmuring something I can't make out. His body seeks mine, even now. Like it's instinct. Like it's always been this way.

And maybe that's why I feel myself slipping. Because deep down, I've always known—we were meant to be.

My chest tightens as I reach for my phone on the nightstand. I read the email again, the words blurring for a second before I take a breath and quietly slip out of bed. Heart hammering, I step into the hallway and call the number at the bottom.

The cemetery is quiet, save for the soft crunch of gravel under my trainers. I didn't bring flowers. I never do. Nico hated them. Said they were for birthdays or breakups.

I find his headstone, the familiar ache blooming in my chest before I even read the inscription;

Nico Salvatore Perelli
Beloved son, brother, friend.
Always the light.

I crouch, brushing away a leaf stuck to the base.

"Hey," I whisper, the word dissolving into the stillness around me. "So, um. Big news."

The silence stretches like I'm waiting for an answer.

"A hotel brand wants to work with me," I say, trying to smile. "Like, my dream hotel brand. Only problem is… I'd be moving to Rome. Like, *actual* Rome. Real pasta, proper wine, tomatoes that actually taste like tomatoes. It's everything I've worked for. Everything I wanted."

My voice falters, just for a second.

"But there's something holding me back. And I think I can finally admit it—to you, to myself..." I brace for the words I've been circling in my mind for as long as I can remember.

"I never told you that I loved him—Charlie—back when we were kids." The words taste strange on my tongue, like I'm scared to say them out loud, like he's judging me from beyond the grave for falling for his best friend. "And I think I still love him. Maybe I never stopped. If he hadn't come back, it wouldn't even be a question. I'd be packing my bags right now." I pause, swallowing. "I know I'd feel guilty leaving Mum and Dad for that long, but... it's been twelve years. I think I can finally let go of needing to protect them."

I swallow hard, pushing down the tangle in my chest.

"You would want me to go. Mum and Dad would too. Olive's already packing my bags in her head.' I smile, just for a second. "You were always rooting for me, even when I had no clue what I was doing."

I tuck a stray piece of hair behind my ear, the air growing cooler against my skin.

"But... Charlie." The name lands like a stone. "I don't know."

I sit, pulling my knees to my chest, letting the quiet fill in all the cracks I don't know how to fix.

"He came back, Nico. And it's not just nostalgia or guilt or whatever the hell I thought it might be. He's here, and it *feels* like something. Like I could maybe stop holding my breath. Let the past go. Let myself be happy."

I exhale slowly.

"But if I stay for him, and he leaves again—or it doesn't work—what then? And if I go... what if I'm walking away from something I'll never find again?"

A breeze rustles the trees, gentle and fleeting. I close my eyes, imagine him rolling his and telling me I'm overthinking it. Again.

"I wish you could tell me what to do," I whisper.

I reach out, fingertips brushing the stone. "I miss you. Every day. But I think... I think it's time I do something for me."

I stand, the decision still sitting heavy in my chest. I walk away, not lighter, not certain—but moving forward all the same.

27

GIA

I Don't Love You

T hree weeks.

That's how long it takes for a dozen phone calls, countless back-and-forth emails, and one impulsive, *holy-shit-am-I-really-doing-this* moment to turn into a booked flight and a packed bag.

First stop? *Roma, baby.*

I should be excited. I *am* excited. But as I stand in the doorway of my childhood bedroom at my parents' house, staring at the suitcase by the door, all I can think about is the warm weight of Charlie's hand on my waist last night. The way he pulled me close in his sleep, instinctively, like he *knew*. Like some part of him already felt me slipping away.

I shake it off. This is my *chance*. My *dream*.

So why does it feel like I'm leaving a piece of myself behind?

And then I think about the night I told him I was leaving.

Charlie was *stoked* for me. Like I'd just won the lottery. Like he was the luckiest person alive to witness my dreams coming true. His whole face lit up, and then he pulled me into one of those tight, full-body hugs—the kind that made me feel like he could hold me together even when I was falling apart.

"Gia, this is huge," he'd said, eyes bright with something that looked a lot like pride. *"You're gonna kill it."*

He's been so *damn* supportive, and it hurts in a way I wasn't ready for.

But I have to do this.

Even if it means leaving him behind.

It's not forever, anyway. We can make the long-distance thing work.

It's only Europe, after all.

The doorbell rings, shaking me out of my thoughts, and then I hear it—*him*. That distinct British-Aussie twang, the voice I've come to know better than my own heartbeat.

The voice I *love*.

Yeah. I love this man with every fibre of my being. And that's how I know this is going to work—*has* to work.

Even if I haven't said it out loud yet.

I linger in the doorway for a moment, savouring the sound of their voices—Charlie, Mum, Dad—chatting in the entryway like this is just any other day. Like I'm not about to board a plane with a one-way ticket and no real plan beyond chasing a dream.

It feels safe. Familiar. It's home.

And maybe that's why I stay frozen here, gripping the doorframe, listening to the way Charlie's laugh blends so easily with my dad's, the way my mum fusses over him like he's already part of the family.

Like he *belongs* here.

Like I do, too.

But I can't let that stop me.

I take a grounding breath, square my shoulders, and grab the handle of my suitcase. One step at a time. That's all this is. Just walking down the stairs. Just heading toward my future.

But as I descend, the sight waiting for me in the entryway knocks the air from my lungs.

Charlie, standing there, bright eyes, mussed hair. His hands tucked into the pockets of his hoodie, his easy smile aimed at my mum as she chatters away. My dad nodding along, already half won over—like Charlie isn't just some guy I used to know, but something *more*. Something unspoken.

Something I'm about to leave behind.

I tighten my grip on the suitcase handle and push the thought away.

Not forever. Just for now.

Charlie clocks me, eyes crinkling with amusement as I wrestle with the monstrosity that's half my size—stuffed with home comforts and a bunch of things I probably won't even need.

"You moving to Europe or smuggling the beach?" he teases, already reaching for the handle before I can protest.

I let him take it. Maybe because I'm tired. Maybe because I just like the way it looks—his big, capable hands carrying a piece of my world like it's nothing.

Or maybe because, deep down, I wish he could carry *all* of this for me. The excitement. The fear. The part of me that wonders if I'm making the right choice.

But this is mine to bear. I owe this to myself. To Nico.

"Shut up," I mutter, nudging his side as I step past him. "You're just jealous I can fit more outfits than you."

"Damn, look at you. Success went straight to your head, huh?"

I shoot him a warning look, but honestly, all I really want to do is kiss him and smuggle *him* into my luggage.

Dad grabs my case and heads outside with it. Mum follows behind, giving Charlie and me a rare moment alone. It feels strange—bittersweet, even—that the last time we were here, in this house, *completely* alone, Nico was still alive.

"Come here," I say, pulling him closer for a kiss before leading him up the stairs.

"G, I'm not defiling you in your parent's house. I'm a classy guy."

"Shut up, you're a slut." I retort, grabbing his hand and dragging him upstairs.

"Only because you made me one," he mutters under his breath.

I stifle a laugh.

When we reach the threshold of Nico's room, Charlie tenses, his body going rigid as if he's preparing for something. I know exactly what he's feeling.

"G, I haven't been in here since..." His voice trails off, and I can feel the weight of what he's not saying—*since he was alive.*

"I know," I say softly, squeezing his hand, trying to ground us both. "Would you mind if I show you something."

Reluctantly, he nods. I take a deep breath, open the door, and step inside.

Everything is exactly as I left it the last time I was here, just as I expected. Neither of my parents have stepped foot in this room except to dust and vacuum. Nico's memory is never disturbed.

I kneel beside the bed and reach under, fingers brushing past dust and forgotten things until I find the box. I pull it out gently and place it on the mattress. Then I sit down, careful not to disturb the quiet.

Being in here always feels sacred, I'd never want to disrespect his space.

Charlie lingers in the doorway for a moment, hands stuffed in the pockets of his hoodie, eyes searching mine. Then, slowly, he steps forward and sits beside me, close enough that the box sits right between us.

"Open it," I say, my voice steady but soft, trying to keep the weight of this moment from cracking me.

Charlie hesitates for a beat, his fingers hovering over the lid. Then, slowly, he lifts it. The faint sound of the cardboard scraping echoes in the quiet room. His eyes flick over the items, the photos, the tickets, pausing on each one, before settling on something buried at the bottom. He pulls out a small, worn leather bracelet.

I watch his expression shift—something between sadness and reverence—as he traces the edges of the bracelet with his thumb.

"He was always wearing this." His voice is barely a whisper, like he's not sure if he's allowed to say it out loud.

I nod, the lump in my throat making it hard to speak.

Charlie looks at me, his expression unreadable for a moment, before his gaze drops to the bracelet. "I remember when he bought it," he says, his voice thick with memory. "We were... fourteen, maybe? He insisted we both get one. Said it was to 'seal our fate,' or some shit. I didn't even want it at first, but he made me."

His eyes linger on the worn leather, the past coming alive in his voice. "Mine broke years ago, though. Lost it in a stupid fight we had..." He trails off, the weight of that memory pulling at him.

"I think you should have it," I say quietly.

"G... I can't," he says, his voice rough, like the weight of the offer is too much for him to carry. But the way his fingers close around the bracelet suggests otherwise.

"You don't have to take it right now..."

"No, it's not that." His voice is rough, like it's scraping against something raw. "I can't... I don't know if I can do this."

My heart aches. My reason crumbles under the weight of his stare. The unspoken grief, the history pressing between us.

"What if I can't let you go?" he says, finally.

And then, silence.

I don't press, allowing him to continue when he's ready.

"I keep telling myself I'll be okay with this. That you're going to do something amazing, and I'll be proud of you, and I'll let you go. But I can't." His voice cracks, and he shakes his head. "I can't let you go, G. I've been trying so damn hard to be strong for you, to be happy for you, but every time I think about you in Rome, my stomach fucking twists. It feels like I'm suffocating.' He exhales sharply, like the confession has knocked the wind out of him. "And I know it's selfish, I know it's not fair, but I can't do this. I can't watch you walk away from me."

My stomach coils, my chest tight. "What? I don't understand." My voice wobbles, the words barely making it past the lump in my throat. "You've been so supportive of this—of my future. You know how much I've wanted this, how hard I've worked. I've *earned* this."

I blink at him, stunned, searching his face for something that makes this make sense. "Why are you telling me this now?"

He swallows hard. "You've worked so hard for this, and you deserve it. But the truth is... I've been selfish this whole time." His jaw clenches, frustration bleeding into his voice. "I've been pretending I can let you go, but I don't want to. I don't want to be the one standing here, watching you chase your dreams while I'm stuck here. Alone."

He exhales sharply, running a hand through his hair. "I can't even picture you in a city so far away, meeting new people, changing. I don't want you to change." His voice drops lower, rough with emotion. "And that makes me the asshole who can't get his shit together."

I can't believe what I'm hearing. How could he be so... *selfish*? After everything.

"Don't do this, Charlie. Don't make me choose." My voice is barely above a whisper, but the weight of it is crushing.

His jaw tightens. "I'm not trying to, G." He drags a hand through his hair, exhaling sharply. "But fuck, I don't know how to do this. How to be okay with this. With you leaving. With me staying."

I shake my head, my heart pounding. "You've been so supportive this whole time. Why are you saying this *now*?"

His eyes darken with something I can't quite name—something *wrecked*. "Because I thought I could handle it. I thought I could be the guy who tells you to chase your dreams and lets you go without falling apart." He laughs, but there's no humour in it. "Turns out, I can't."

"So what are you saying?" My voice wavers, and I hate it. Hate how small I feel in this moment.

Charlie swallows hard, his gaze flickering to the bracelet still clenched in his fist. "I don't know." He exhales, shaking his head. "That I don't want you to go. That I don't know who I am without you. That I'm scared if you leave, I'll just be this... hollow version of myself, waiting for something that isn't coming back."

I close my eyes, trying to steady myself, trying not to let his words dig under my skin and plant doubt. But they do. Of course they do.

"You can't say this to me now." I whisper it, but it feels like a scream. "Not when I'm about to leave. Not when I've spent so long convincing myself that you—" I cut myself off before the rest of the thought can slip out.

That he never wanted me like this. That I was always alone in this longing.

But now? Now he's making it impossible to leave without feeling like I'm breaking something we never even let ourselves have.

My voice is barely above a whisper, but it cuts through the silence like a blade. "I think you should go."

Charlie flinches, like I've physically struck him. "G..."

"Please." I look away, blinking rapidly, trying to hold it together. "I can't do this right now. I need you to leave before I say something I'll regret."

For a second, he doesn't move. The tension in the air thickens as he seems to weigh my words, trying to figure out what to do. Then, without another word, he places the bracelet back in the box, his fingers lingering on it for a second too long before he stands, turns, walks away.

And just like that, he's gone. Out of my life.

Again.

28

CHARLIE

All That I've Got

T he latch clicks, final and hollow, and I stand there for a beat, hand still on the handle, like maybe if I stay still long enough, time will, too.

But it doesn't. Of course it fucking doesn't.

I'm the biggest asshole there is.

I deserve everything that's coming to me.

My feet feel like lead as I head downstairs. Each step creaks louder than it should, like the house is protesting. Like even it knows I don't want to go.

Gia's folks are by the front door, luggage already in the boot. Mrs P looks up, smiling gently—until she sees my face. The smile falters.

"Charlie?" she asks softly. "Everything okay?"

I force a nod. My throat is tight, but the words come out even. "She's just grabbing something from upstairs. She'll be down in a sec."

It's not a lie, not exactly. But I can't stay here a second longer.

Mr P gives me a polite nod, but his eyes linger a little too long, like he's trying to read between the lines. I don't let him.

"I should get going," I say quickly, my voice scraping out like gravel.

Gia's mum reaches out, touching my arm briefly. "Take care of yourself, love."

I nod again. Swallow the ache. "You too. All of you."

And then I'm out the door, sucking in a sharp breath of sea air like it might shock something back into place. It doesn't. I walk fast, not trusting myself to look back. Not trusting myself *at all*.

Because if she called out my name right now, even once—I don't think I'd make it past the front gate.

29

GIA

If It Means a Lot to You

The car's too quiet.

Mum keeps sneaking glances at me through the rearview mirror, like she's waiting for me to say something, to *break*. Dad drums his fingers against the steering wheel, humming along to whatever the hell is playing on the radio like he'd rather be anywhere else. Or maybe he just doesn't want to get involved. Not that I can blame him.

I press my forehead to the glass, watching the houses blur past, everything familiar turning into a goodbye.

My chest aches. Not the sharp, punch-to-the-gut kind of ache. No, this is worse. This is that slow, creeping, hollow pain—the kind that spreads out behind your ribs and sinks its teeth in, the kind that whispers, *you did the right thing*, while your heart screams, *then why does it hurt this much?*

No one says Charlie's name.

Not even me.

But I feel him in every mile we put between us. In the bracelet tucked in my pocket. In the ghost of his touch on my skin. In the words I should have said, but didn't.

The distance won't change a thing.

I love him. Despite everything.

Yeah, no shit.

Doesn't change the fact that he ruined everything. And I fell for it.

Again.

I swallow hard and blink up at the roof of the car like maybe I can stop the tears from falling just by sheer force of will.

I wanted this. I worked for this. Rome, the sponsorship, the dream I've clung to for so long. And now I've got it. All of it.

So why do I feel like I just left something behind I'll never get back?

The terminal is bright and buzzing, but it all feels muted. Like I'm underwater. Or in a dream I'm not ready to wake up from.

We're standing near the check-in desk, and Mum keeps adjusting my outfit like I'm five years old again. Her hands are trembling.

"You've got everything?" she asks for the third time.

I nod. "Yeah."

"Passport?"

"Yeah."

"Charger?"

"Mum." I give her a small, wobbly smile. "I've got it."

She presses her lips together like she's trying not to cry. I can tell she's debating whether to say something meaningful or just let the moment pass without it cracking open too wide.

Dad clears his throat beside her, awkward and stiff. "You'll message when you land, yeah?"

"Of course."

A pause. Just long enough for the air to get heavy.

"We're proud of you," Mum whispers. Her voice is thick. "So proud."

I swallow the lump in my throat. "Thanks."

She hugs me, tight and unyielding. Then Dad does too, in that way he does—brief but strong. A steady presence, even now.

None of us say Charlie's name.

I want to. I want to ask if they spoke to him, or if he just up and left without saying goodbye—he's good at that.

But I can't. Because if I do, I'll fall apart. And my emotions can't afford that right now.

So I pick up my suitcase and turn toward the gate.

One step. Then another.

Don't look back, Gia.

Just keep going.

The crowd shifts as I near the security barrier, a blur of movement and noise. I keep my eyes down, focused on the tiled floor, the wheels of my suitcase clicking steadily behind me.

And then—

A flicker.

Just ahead, over by the café. Dirty blonde hair, tousled and familiar. Broad shoulders in a navy hoodie.

My heart lurches. Stops. Starts again.

It's not him.

Of course it's not him.

But for half a second, my body doesn't know the difference. It reacts anyway. Like a ghost of a feeling. Like muscle memory.

One step. Then another.

I don't let myself stop walking.

Just keep going, Gia.

This is what you wanted. What you worked for.

The overhead announcement calls my flight. Final boarding.

I don't look back again.

The city hums beyond the tarmac—warm, unfamiliar—as a golden haze stretches across the runway at Fiumicino Airport.

A whole new life, waiting to be lived.

The wave of heat hits me the moment I step off the plane. Board the shuttle.

I move on autopilot through customs, claim my bag, and step into the arrivals hall, where the air feels thicker—warmer—buzzing with languages I only half understand. It should feel overwhelming.

But instead... it's quiet.

Inside me, at least. The kind of quiet that comes after a storm.

My phone buzzes with a dozen missed messages—some from the team here, a few from Mum, Olive... and one from Charlie.

I don't open it. Not yet.

My Rome-bound PA is already waiting for me at the arrivals gate, standing tall in his tailored black suit like he stepped off the set of an old film. His jawline is so sharp it could probably slice prosciutto, and his dark hair is slicked back with just enough wave to look perfectly undone.

"Signorina Gia," he says, voice warm and accented in all the right ways. "Benvenuta. I'm Luigi." He flashes a grin that could make a nun forget her vows, and I blink, momentarily stunned. He might be the most beautiful man I've ever seen.

He air-kisses me on both cheeks, catching me off guard. Then he takes my suitcase with practiced ease and gestures to the sleek black car idling outside. "Shall we?"

The whole ride into the city feels like a dream—like the version of Rome you see in the movies. Warm light spilling across cobbled streets. Vespas weaving through traffic. People sitting outside shops and trattoria, smoking cigarettes, chatting and laughing. Easy. Effortless.

"You're going to love Trastevere," he says, humming along to the song on the radio.

We drive past the Malfi Roma—the Luxe's sister hotel, and I actually gasp. It's dripping with luxury. But the deeper we go, the dream starts to fray a little.

Trastevere is beautiful, no doubt—but it's also rougher around the edges than I expected. The buildings are old and charming, sure—but the graffiti sprawled across the walls feels like a personal attack. The streets are narrower here, the cobblestones uneven, and everything smells just a little too much like motor oil and cigarette smoke.

A flicker of unease twists in my stomach.

This isn't the glossy Roman fantasy The Lustre Collection promised.

When Luigi slows the car down a tight alleyway and stops in front of a small, vine-draped building, my heart lurches. It's... charming, sure. Traditional Italian architecture, faded shutters, climbing flowers. But it's also small. Tired-looking. And not exactly what I pictured when I thought *luxury culinary residency.*

I hesitate, my hand frozen halfway to the door handle. For a wild second, I consider asking him to take me back to the airport. Maybe Rome was a mistake. Maybe all of this was a mistake.

Luigi catches my expression in the mirror and smiles—a small, knowing thing, like he's seen it a hundred times before.

"Wait there, Signorina," he says, unbuckling his seatbelt and stepping out. He circles around to open my door with a flourish, offering his hand like we're about to walk into a ballroom instead of an alleyway. "The Malfi Roma is beautiful. But the Malfi Luxe?" He flashes a grin. "That's the magic. Trust me."

I stare at him for a beat. His confidence isn't pushy—it's easy, gentle, like he's offering me a hand across a river instead of shoving me into it.

I trail after Luigi as he wheels my suitcase over the uneven cobblestones.

The alleyway is narrow, hemmed in by crumbling plaster walls splashed with graffiti. Vines crawl up the sides of weathered buildings, trying to hold it all together. For a second, I wonder if I've been sold a dream, if all the glossy Instagram posts had cropped out the grime.

The air smells like a strange mix of garlic and car exhaust, something sweet and citrusy layered over the scent of baking. The moment I catch it—whatever's fresh out of the oven—my stomach twists.

Because it makes me think of Charlie. And he's the last person I need on my mind right now.

Somewhere close by, a guitar strums a lazy tune. As we reach the door of the Malfi Luxe, Luigi glances back at me, catching my expression. "Wait until you see it," he says, smiling. At this point, I'm putting all of my faith in this man.

I follow him—and my now-battered suitcase—through the arched doorway into the cool, shaded lobby of the Malfi Luxe. Stone floors gleam underfoot. The scent of lemon blossoms hangs in the air. And just beyond the sweeping reception desk, a glass elevator rises toward a rooftop I can't quite see yet.

Luigi glances back over his shoulder, eyes glinting. "Ready to fall in love with Rome?"

I square my shoulders and step inside.

"Don't I need to check in first?" I ask.

"Don't worry. I've already checked you in and made sure your suite has everything you need—including bottomless espresso," he says with a wink, pulling something out of his pocket and handing it to me. "This is your key card, just swipe it right here," he says, gesturing towards a receiver on the elevator.

We step inside, and the elevator glides upward with a soft hum, my heart beating louder with every floor we pass.

Luigi stands beside me, still holding my suitcase like it weighs nothing, wearing the patient smile of a man who knows the secret at the end of the story.

When the doors open, sunlight pours inside, blinding and golden. I squint, stepping out onto warm stone tiles—and the world falls away.

The rooftop stretches wide and open around me, framed by low stone walls wrapped in ivy. A turquoise pool shimmers at the centre, so clear it looks almost surreal against the weathered tiles. Elegant white loungers are scattered around, half shaded by linen umbrellas that flutter lazily in the breeze.

But it's the view that steals my breath.

Beyond the rooftop, Rome spills out in every direction—a chaos of rooftops, terracotta and cream, stitched together with narrow streets and sudden bursts of green. The Tiber River glints like a silver ribbon winding through the city, and on the horizon, domes and spires pierce the sky—ancient and eternal. I spot the unmistakable silhouette of St. Peter's Basilica, the marble monument of Piazza Venezia, and beyond that, the hint of the Colosseum's battered, beautiful curve.

The city hums below, alive and golden and mine, at least for a little while.

A laugh bubbles up in my throat, light and unexpected. I press a hand to my chest, feeling the thrum of possibility all over again.

Luigi sets down my bag and gestures toward a table tucked under a canopy of climbing jasmine, where a chilled bottle of prosecco sweats in an ice bucket, two glasses waiting.

"Welcome to Malfi Luxe," he says, with a wink that somehow manages to be both cheeky and sweet. "Told you it was magic."

I smile, because it feels like the right thing to do. Because I *should* be smiling. It stretches across my face like muscle memory—but there's no real joy in it. Just the shape of what joy's supposed to look like.

"Yeah," I say, my voice barely holding steady. "You really did."

Fall in love with Rome?

Of course I have. How could I not?

The colours, the air, the light—it's all impossibly beautiful.

But something in me stays stubbornly grey.

Because he's not here.

Charlie.

The person I want to share this with. The one I imagined beside me.

And I hate that I can't just be *grateful*, can't just be *present*.

But how do you feel whole in a place like this when your heart's somewhere else?

My one true love?

He's back home.

And I'm here, chasing magic with someone who isn't him.

30

GIA

Blue and Yellow

Later that evening, after I finally shower the plane ride off me and pretend to unpack, Luigi meets me downstairs in the lobby. He's swapped his suit for beige chinos and a white button-down, sleeves shoved up to his elbows. The whole fit is classic. Effortless. Like he's stepped off the cover of Italian Vogue. Not a damn hair out of place.

"Come on," he says, grinning. "I want you to meet my fiancée. We're getting an aperitivo. You can't come to Rome and hide in your hotel."

I hesitate, glancing out at the narrowing twilight, the city blurring into pinks and golds. The safe option is saying no. Staying in my room. Ordering room service and scrolling Instagram like a ghost haunting my own life.

But something about Luigi—his easy confidence, his warm eyes—pushes me to nod. "Okay. Just for a little while."

He claps his hands together like I've just agreed to elope with him. "Perfetto!"

The streets are cooling down, but the air still smells like warm stone and roasted garlic. We weave through alleyways strung with fairy lights, past laundry flapping from high windows. The square comes into view, pulsing with music and life.

Luigi's fiancée is waiting by the fountain. She's gorgeous, of course, all sun-kissed skin and effortless curls, wearing a gauzy white dress like she floated straight out of a movie scene. They kiss in a way that makes me look away, pretending to be fascinated by a neon Aperol sign.

Anything to ignore the way my chest caves in.

The music starts—a rough, happy kind of sound—and they start dancing, messy and sweet, right there in the square. Other couples join them. A few tourists too. It's clumsy, beautiful chaos.

And it feels like the universe twisting the knife. Instead, I tell myself it's all a show. A pretty little performance for tourists who want to believe in magic.

I wrap my arms around myself, squeezing tight. Watching them stings in a way I wasn't ready for. Because I had that once. But Charlie is a whole ocean away now. Out of reach. Maybe always was.

How am I supposed to get over him all over again?

I don't want a spritz. I don't want pasta. I want to go home.

But home is gone too.

So I stand there, pretending the sunset isn't blurring in my eyes. Pretending the music isn't rattling something broken inside me. Pretending, pretending, pretending.

I order an overpriced spritz, lean against a crumbling wall, and let the music thrum against my ribs. Trying not to want more.

My finger hovers over Charlie's unopened message. Just one tap. Just one glimpse.

But before I can do it, my phone vibrates in my hand. Incoming call.

Olive.

For a second, I just stare at her name flashing on the screen, my heart beating out a stubborn, miserable rhythm.

I could ignore it. I could pretend I'm already halfway home. I could throw the phone into the goddamn Tiber and watch it sink.

Instead, I answer.

"Hey," I say, my voice scraping out rough and low.

"You made it!" Olive says, bright and hopeful, like if she just wills it hard enough, I'll suddenly be having the time of my life.

Like she doesn't know me at all. Or maybe she knows me too well.

I sink down onto the edge of a cracked stone planter, the air heavy with cigarette smoke and the salty tang of pizza dough. "Yeah," I say. "I'm here."

A beat of silence. "You sound like you're having fun," she teases gently.

I close my eyes. "Ols, it's... not what I thought it would be." The words scrape out before I can stop them, shame thick in my throat. "I think I made a mistake."

Another beat. Then Olive says, steady and sure, "It's not a mistake. It's just the beginning."

"You always say that," I murmur, picking at a loose thread on my dress.

"Because it's true," Olive says, stubborn. "You just need to give it a chance. Rome isn't magic the second you step off the plane. You have to let it get under your skin first."

I huff a soft, humourless laugh. "What if I don't want it under my skin?"

What if the only thing under my skin is still him?

"You do," Olive says quietly. "You just don't want to yet."

The words land harder than they should. I swallow, my throat burning. "Maybe I should just come home."

"No," Olive says, sharp enough to slice through the heavy heat pressing down on me. "Gia. You're allowed to be miserable. You're allowed to miss him. But you're not allowed to quit before you even fucking try."

I blink hard at the cracked cobblestones, blinking against the sting in my eyes. "I didn't come here to cry in the middle of the street," I mutter.

"No, you went there to live."

I open my mouth to argue—to say something mean and defensive—but then a warm voice cuts through the thick air.

"There she is!"

I look up. Luigi is striding toward me, a beautiful woman at his side.

Her smile is easy. She's laughing at something Luigi just said, her hand looped through his arm, effortlessly casual. They look like they belong here, in this sun-drenched, crumbling postcard of a city.

I don't.

"Talk to you later," I say into the phone, before Olive can answer. I hang up without waiting for her goodbye.

I plaster on my best fake smile, hoping that neither of them can see through it.

"Gia, this is Rosa," Luigi beams, clearly proud. "My fiancée."

Rosa leans in immediately, pressing a kiss to each of my cheeks like we're old friends. Her perfume is light and floral, wrapping around me as easily as her arms do.

"It's so good to meet you!" she says in warm, accented English. "Luigi told me you were nervous about coming to Rome. Don't worry, we'll take care of you."

I swallow, the knot in my throat tight as ever. "Thank you," I manage, my voice steady but flat.

"Come," Rosa says brightly, looping her arm through mine. "You must dance with us! You can't be sad in Trastevere. It's forbidden!"

I hesitate, feeling the weight of the night pressing on me, the distance from everything I know, the ache that never quite goes away. I take a step back, smiling a little too stiffly.

"Honestly, I'm just... I'm so jet-lagged," I say, rubbing my temple lightly.

Luigi's smile falters just a bit, but his gaze softens when he sees the exhaustion in my eyes. "Of course, Gia," he says kindly, though I can tell he's trying to hide his disappointment. "We'll let you rest."

"Yeah, you two go on and have fun," I say, offering them both a polite, though strained, smile.

Rosa presses her lips together, sensing my reluctance, but nods in understanding. "Alright, but next time," she insists, winking. "We'll dance for you."

I give them a small wave, then turn and walk away, the weight of the square, the music, the laughter, all pulling at me in a way I can't explain. It's not that I don't want to be part of it, I just can't. Not tonight.

As I slip down the alley, away from the music and the people, I feel a tightness in my chest, a loneliness that wraps around me like a shadow I can't shake.

But I can't think of that now. Not with Charlie still haunting every corner of my mind.

So I walk faster, my heart a little more broken with every step as I will the tears not to fall.

But they do. Of course they do.

Back in my room at the Malfi Luxe, I sit on the edge of the bed, the city's distant hum filtering through the shuttered windows. The suitcase lies untouched in the corner, a silent reminder of the life I'm supposed to be starting.

My phone rests beside me, Charlie's message still unopened. I tell myself it's better this way, that reading it won't change anything. But the questions linger: What is he doing? Is he thinking about me?

I shake my head, trying to dispel the thoughts. Dwelling won't help. Not tonight.

I lie back, staring at the ceiling, the unfamiliarity of the room pressing in. Sleep feels distant, but I close my eyes anyway, hoping for rest.

I've survived worse.

Tomorrow is just another day.

Rome is waiting for me when I wake up, along with a string of messages from Olive. I don't deserve her. Even from across the pond, she's still my own personal cheerleader.

I was harsh last night. I shoot off a quick apology, promise I'll call her later when I'm less of a misery.

A text from Luigi pings through next, outlining today's schedule. Apparently, I'm meeting the kitchen team this morning—getting a behind-the-scenes look at their plant-based options, maybe even throwing a few dishes together if I'm feeling brave. There's a rooftop garden tour after that, and a tasting session where I'm meant to snap a million photos and make it all look effortless.

Then the afternoon's mine. The whole of Rome at my feet. No pressure or anything.

And yet all I can think about is a boy back home.

31

CHARLIE

Kissing in Cars

I hand my keys back to the manager at Six with a smile that doesn't quite reach. It's not goodbye. Not officially. They're keeping the door open for me if I ever want to come back. But it *feels* like goodbye.

I walk past the front windows without looking in. I can't bear to see it. The quiet kitchen. The empty tables. The ghost of the life I thought I was building here. Maybe it's time to go back to Australia. Maybe it's time to stop pretending I can make a life here without her. Without *them*. Without all the pieces I lost along the way.

I pull my hoodie up over my head and duck down a side street, trying to outrun the weight sitting on my chest. It's been zero days since my last panic attack.

Zero fucking days. I should start a tally on my fridge or something. Make a joke out of it before it eats me alive.

I press the heels of my hands into my eyes and breathe deep, the way I've learned to.

Feet on the ground. Eyes closed. Ears open. Breathe in. Breathe out. You're here. You're safe.

But all I smell is rain and car exhaust. All I hear is the ache of everything I can't fix. I'm trying. God knows I'm trying.

I cut through the alley behind Six, feet scuffing the slick pavement, hands jammed deep into my pockets like I can physically hold myself together if I try hard enough.

Maybe I should call Jules, one of my buddies back home. He said there's a spot at his place if I want it. Surf lessons and shitty coffee and sunsets that almost make the broken parts of me quiet down.

But it feels like quitting. Feels like running. Feels like every time I pack a bag and get on a plane, I'm leaving more pieces of myself scattered in the dirt behind me.

I don't know how to stay. I don't know how to leave.

I stop under an awning when the rain gets heavier, drag in a breath so sharp it burns the back of my throat. It doesn't help.

Nothing helps.

My hands are shaking. I turn them over in front of me like I'm surprised to see it—like I'm a stranger inside my own skin. My therapist says the body remembers. Trauma sits in the bones, waiting. I think mine's been waiting for this moment all along.

The keys rattle in my pocket. A goodbye and a lifeline all at once. The temptation to hurl them into the gutter is so strong I have to physically turn my body away from the road.

I'm supposed to be better than this. I'm supposed to be healing.

But the truth is, it's been zero fucking days since I felt like I was drowning in a life that doesn't fit me anymore. Since I started wondering if maybe I'm the one thing I can't fix.

I squeeze my eyes shut. Try to find the ground again. Rain. The damp stink of wet brick. The low growl of a bus rumbling past.

But all I can think about is her.

Her laugh, low and warm in the back of her throat. The way she looks at me like I was never broken at all.

I shove off the wall and start walking, nowhere in particular. Just moving, because if I stop, I'll fall apart. And if I fall apart, I'm not sure I'll know how to put myself back together this time.

I don't even realise where my feet are taking me until the bright, greasy warmth of a little pizza joint punches through the rain.

Tiny place. Handwritten specials board half smeared from the humidity. Window steamed up so bad I can't see inside, but the door's half open, like it's daring me to step through.

I hover. Drenched. Shaking. Fucking pathetic.

But inside it's warm. Inside it smells like bread and tomatoes and the kind of cheap cheese that sticks to the roof of your mouth.

And it's not Six. It's not empty tables and the ghost of a life that didn't work out.

So I go in.

The bell above the door gives a weak little jingle, and a kid behind the counter looks up. Barely old enough to shave.

"Eat in or takeaway?" he asks, voice bored in the way only teenagers can manage.

I blink at him. I don't even know. I don't even know what the fuck I'm doing anymore. "Eat in," I say finally, voice rough. "Please."

He nods, taps a laminated menu against the counter. I take it without really looking, drop into a sticky vinyl booth by the window.

My hoodie squelches against the seat. I'm dripping onto the floor. I should care more than I do.

I rub my hands over my face. Try to catch my breath.

Zero days. Zero fucking days.

Maybe Australia isn't the answer. Maybe nothing is. Maybe the whole point is that there *isn't* an answer.

The kid brings over a glass of water without me asking. Just dumps it down and wanders off again. I wrap my hands around it like it'll tether me to the world for a second longer.

I stare out at the rain and wonder how the hell you're supposed to rebuild a life when you don't even know what you're building towards anymore.

The kid comes back a few minutes later, a plate in one hand, phone in the other. He's half-watching a video, earbuds dangling loose.

"Sorry, bro," he says, sliding the plate in front of me without really looking. "We're outta mozzarella, so I just, like... made it work."

I glance down. It's not what I ordered. Not even close. Some Frankenstein mess of pepperoni, feta, and what looks suspiciously like pineapple.

Normally, it would piss me off. Today, it just... doesn't.

I nod. "Thanks."

The kid flashes a quick, sheepish smile before slouching back behind the counter.

I pick up a slice. The cheese stretches and snaps, oily and ridiculous. It burns the roof of my mouth when I take a bite.

It tastes like shit. It tastes amazing. It tastes like something real.

I sit there, chewing, rain smearing the world outside into a blur of grey and neon. Maybe I don't have to figure it all out tonight. Maybe I don't have to figure it all out at all.

Maybe surviving today is enough.

I take another bite. And for the first time in what feels like a long time, I don't feel like I'm drowning.

I'm halfway through another slice when my phone pings, screen lighting up against the sticky red of the table.

My heart jerks so hard it hurts. It's stupid, how fast I hope. How fast I always hope.

Maybe it's her. Maybe it's Gia. Maybe she—

It's not.

It's my dad. I let it ring off, then, a minute later, I get a message.

> *Dad: Give us a call, mate. Heard on the grapevine you're thinking about coming home.*

I stare at the message until the words blur.

Home.

Where even is home anymore?

I shake my head.

Sure, I'll come back *home*—not to try again. Not for a fresh fucking start.

I'm going back to close it down. Pack up the business. Box up the life I built like it was supposed to save me. Sell the apartment I thought would be full of love and laughter and all the things I was too scared to want out loud.

Because it's not home anymore.

Because nothing feels like home anymore.

I drag the pizza plate toward me, suddenly starving and hollow all at once.

I don't reply.

I don't call.

I just... endure.

I shove my phone away from me and finish eating like it's some kind of penance.

The rain eases up outside. But it still feels like it's pouring inside me.

And then, I do the unthinkable.

I open Instagram. Hands shaking. Heart already punishing me for it. Then, without thinking, I type her handle into the search bar.

The first reel auto-plays — her "first day in Rome."

I watch it without breathing.

She's sitting at a little table outside a crumbling, sun-baked café, glass of Aperol in one hand, sunglasses pushed up into her hair. There's a plate of pasta in front of her, messy and beautiful. Another clip—her laughing over a tray of bright, perfect veggie dishes. Another—a pizza sliding onto a table, thin and charred and about a million times better than the greasy mess I'm hopelessly shoving into my mouth.

She looks... happy.

At least, she wants to.

She's so good at it. At looking happy. At pretending it doesn't hurt.

A knot forms in my chest. I did that—I made it harder for her to leave. I unloaded everything on her, all my messy, too-late feelings, when she was supposed to be excited, supposed to feel free walking onto that plane. She deserved that, and I took it from her.

Maybe I'm not the only one who sees the sadness behind her eyes—I'm not arrogant enough to think that. But I do see it. Clear as day. Always have.

There's this one night I always go back to. The first time I saw her. Met her.

It was years ago. Some dingy club, walls sweating with bass, everyone drunk on cheap lager and teenage recklessness. Nico had dragged me there, swore the next band was going to be the next big thing. I barely remember the music. I remember *her*.

Jet-black hair flying. Wild and reckless in the mosh pit. She was small but unshakeable—laughing in the face of a guy twice her size who shoved too hard. I thought she was about to get crushed. I tried to help.

"Hey—you might want to move back a bit."

She'd spun on me, eyes blazing. "I think I can handle myself, thanks."

And fuck, could she ever.

I stood there, dumbstruck, watching her fight for her place in the chaos like she was born in it. I couldn't look away. Not even when Nico came back from the bar. Not even when the set ended and the house lights came up.

Outside, under buzzing streetlamps, she was all smirks and sarcasm. Called me a fucking buzzkill. Then Nico said her name—and the floor shifted beneath me.

Gia. *His* Gia.

I felt like the biggest joke alive. And maybe I've felt that way ever since.

I see the way her fingers twitch against the table, like she's reminding herself to stay still. I see the second-too-long pause before she laughs. And fuck it if I haven't always seen her.

Before I can talk myself out of it, my thumb hovers over the message button.

Every instinct I have screams at me to close the app. To run. To protect what little pride I have left.

But instead—I hit "message."

She still hasn't responded. Still hasn't even *read* the last message I sent her.

The one where I apologised. The one where I poured my fucking heart out, expecting something—anything. And nothing. Not even a notification.

I scroll back through it. My thumb hovers over her name like it's a mistake, like opening that thread is going to open a wound I'm not sure I can close again.

The words I sent her are so fucking raw, I can taste them in the back of my throat.

I read them again.

Every. Single. Word.

I stare at it. Wonder if it sounds as pathetic as it feels. Wonder if she just thought I was some chump chasing ghosts when I was trying to chase her—trying to make things right. I don't know what's worse; being left on *read*, or being completely fucking ignored.

I slam my phone down on the table like it's the source of all my problems. But it's not. It's just the latest.

I used to think I was the one who got left behind. But now? Now, I'm just fucking angry at the world again.

The kind of anger that pushes everything into sharp focus. The kind that burns up the soft edges of all my thoughts.

It's not a pit of despair anymore. Now, it's a fire. A burning, fucked-up rage.

Maybe I had it coming. Maybe it's been building up for twelve years, ever since I *left*. I walked out on her. Walked out on *us*. And now karma's come back to bite me in the ass.

I deserve everything I'm getting.

I push the rest of the pizza away. The slice looks greasy and sad now, just like me. I'm not hungry anymore. Not for this. Not for anything.

I stare at it for a beat longer than I should, like I'm trying to decide if I'm disappointed in myself or in the pizza. Either way, I'm not eating another bite.

The weight of it all settles back into my chest, heavy and unshakable. I grab my phone again my fingers trembling, but this time it's not to scroll mindlessly or hope for something I know won't come. It's time to book a flight.

It's time to go back to Australia. To pack up. To close it all down.

I can't keep pretending this life—the one I tried to build—is anything but a fucking dead end.

I pull up the flight app, my thumb hovering over dates, prices, destinations. I don't care how much it costs. I don't care about anything except leaving this town, this place, this version of my life behind.

I'm not sure what's worse—the fact that I can't stop thinking about her, or the fact that I know I'm about to make the biggest fucking mistake of my life.

But it's done. It's decided.

I hit 'book' before I can talk myself out of it. And just like that, I'm on my way back to a life that never really felt like mine.

32

GIA

The Ghost of You

A few days pass, a week. Life in Rome is starting to feel... easier.

Luigi and Rosa have been nothing short of amazing, taking me under their wings like I'm part of the family. The food here—Jesus, the food—has been transcendent. Each meal feels like a gift, like a love letter from the earth to my soul. Pasta that melts in your mouth, pizza that tastes like heaven. Everything tastes like love, like home. Even when I can't quite claim a place as *home* anymore.

I've spent hours exploring, losing myself in the winding streets, in the echoes of history that hum through every cracked wall and ancient monument. The Sistine Chapel almost made me forget to breathe, the art so beautiful it made my skin tingle. For a moment, I almost believed the ache inside me might fade into the backdrop of all this magnificence.

But it doesn't. It never does. There's still that hole. That empty space inside me that's been there for so long, I don't even know when it first appeared.

I've learned to live with it. I will learn again. Even if it means letting him go. Even if it means pretending like I'm not haunted by the ghost of the man I once thought I'd spend forever with.

I'm trying to move forward, but it's like walking with one foot always dragging behind. I can't help it. The past keeps following me. Keeps pulling at me.

Just as I'm settling into the warmth of the kitchen and the gentle murmur of Italian chatter around me, my phone buzzes. It's Mum.

I swipe to answer, pushing the thoughts of Charlie out of my head, or trying to.

"Hey, Mum," I say, my voice soft but steady. I know she can tell when something's off, but I try to keep it together for her. For both of us.

We talk about the usual stuff—what I've been eating, what monuments I've seen, if I've managed to stay out of trouble. I tell her about my latest adventure to the Pantheon, how the columns looked like giants pushing their way up from the earth, and how the light through the windows made everything shimmer.

She laughs, her voice warm and full of home. There's a subtle shift in her voice that doesn't go unnoticed, right before she drops something unexpected. Something that shatters the fragile peace I've been building.

"Gia... I wasn't sure whether to tell you, but... Charlie's leaving," she says, her voice uncertain, like she's testing the waters.

I freeze. The words hit me like a slap, cold and unexpected. "Wait—what?" I barely recognise my own voice, the panic creeping in before I can stop it. "When?"

"He's going back to Australia," Mum says, her tone still light, casual. "Tonight. Dad's offered to help pack up his things." She doesn't elaborate, but I don't need her to. My parents love Charlie like a son, even after he broke their hearts, too.

This feels like a bad joke, like something out of a dream I didn't want to wake up from.

But it's not a joke. It's the truth. Charlie's leaving. And I don't know how to stop it.

I squeeze my eyes shut, trying to hold back the sting of tears. I didn't think it would hit me like this but it does. It's like everything I thought I knew about us, about what we were, is unravelling in an instant.

I swallow hard, the lump in my throat threatening to choke me. I don't say anything for a long time. Mum's voice cracks through the silence, still trying to be light. "You're going to be okay, sweetheart. You always are."

Am I? Because right now, I feel like I'm drowning in questions I can't answer. Was he ever really mine? Was I ever really his? Did he love me, or was I just something to pass the time before he *left*? Why didn't he tell me? Why didn't he let me say goodbye?

I don't say any of this, though. I don't ask her any of it. I just nod, and she moves on to something else.

But I can't move on from this. From him. From the thought that he's really gone this time.

And as I pull my phone closer to me, staring at his message—*still unread*—I know the worst part. I can't bring myself to open it. Because once I do, I'll have to face the truth.

And maybe that's the one thing I'm not ready for.

33

CHARLIE

You're So Last Summer

"Got everything you need?" Mr P asks, clapping a heavy hand on my shoulder. A good, solid dad pat. The kind that says *I'm proud of you*, even when I don't deserve it.

I nod, swallowing down the guilt that's clawing up my throat.

Gia's folks have always been amazing to me, and how do I repay them for their kindness? By shitting all over it. Over their loyalty. Over their trust. By breaking their daughter's heart. Again.

I force a smile, shove my hands deeper into the pocket of my hoodie. "I'm good, thanks. Appreciate it though."

I don't deserve their kindness. I never did. I know Gia will be fine—hell, better off—without me dragging her down. I'm just too fucking selfish to accept it.

"Take care of yourself, son," he says, before climbing back into his car. The door slams shut with a dull thud, and I just stand there, the word *son* echoing in my chest like a hole I didn't realise needed filling. I blink hard, like that's going to stop the burn behind my eyes. It doesn't. Mr P drives away without looking back. Probably because he knows I won't either.

I stand in front of my temporary home. Even now, I can't bear to be inside. Everywhere I look in that place reminds me of her. Of what I ruined.

A fresh start—that's what I need. Like a cleansing ritual or something. Shame I can't sage my shitty attitude while I'm at it. Or the fact that I've always been a selfish prick. What would Nico think of me right now?

Probably the same thing I think of myself.

I glance up at the sky, even though I'm not even sure what it's supposed to mean.

"I'm sorry, mate," I say, voice rough and low, like maybe if I say it out loud, he'll hear me. Like maybe forgiveness could fall out of the fucking sky if I just ask nicely enough. A hollow laugh slips out before I can stop it.

Nico would probably call me a dumbass for apologising to the clouds.

I shove my hands deeper into my pockets, the cool air biting at my skin.

Who am I kidding? Nico was the most forgiving person I ever knew. He would've forgiven me before I even got the words out. He probably already has. It's me who can't forgive myself.

My throat tightens, the pressure building behind my eyes like I've got the whole damn world sitting on my chest. I try to swallow it down, but it's there. A lump, burning, heavy, making it harder to breathe. I turn my back to the sky, bite my lip, and walk away, hoping the ache doesn't follow.

34

GIA

The Last Song

I sit on the edge of the bed, staring at the cracked screen of my phone like it's personally betrayed me. Charlie's leaving. Going back to Australia. And it feels so... final.

I should have seen it coming. I should have known better than to think this time would be different. But still—it feels like the ground's been ripped out from under me. Like all the work I've been doing to hold myself together just crumbled with one careless sentence from my mum—not that I can blame her.

I think about going to that cute little vegan bakery I found the other day—the one with the pistachio profiteroles that taste like actual heaven. Maybe I should go buy everything they have. Sit cross-legged on my bed, surrounded by pastries, and spiral in peace. Cry into a pile of sugar and pretend like I'm fine. Pretend like I'm not unravelling from the inside out.

But even the thought of moving feels impossible. Everything is heavy. Loud. It's too much.

I scrub my hands over my face and drag myself upright. The walls of my hotel room feel like they're closing in, so I do the only thing I can think of. I grab my key card, shove it into my pocket, and head for the rooftop terrace. Some fresh air might help. Or at the very least, maybe I'll finally dissolve into the sky and be done with it.

I push open the door to the rooftop and walk straight into it. Not peace. Not quiet.

A goddamn wedding.

Of course.

Of course there's a wedding.

The universe isn't even trying to be subtle anymore. It's full-on trolling me. The kind of cruel, cosmic joke that would be hilarious if I wasn't living it.

I stand there, awkward as fuck, while the newlyweds pose for photos against the backdrop of the Roman skyline, all soft golden light and laughter and *forever*. Meanwhile, I'm the disaster in the background, watching someone else's happy ending while mine burns quietly to ash in my chest.

Perfect.

Just fucking perfect.

I grab a free glass of prosecco off a passing tray and try to blend in, like I belong here. Like my heart isn't splintering into a thousand messy pieces. I pick the table furthest from the action and sit down, the glass sweating in my hand, staring at my phone like it might explode. The message is still there. Still unread. Still heavy. It's now or never. I need to know.

My thumb hovers over the screen, shaking like a damn leaf. Just open it, Gia. Rip off the fucking Band-Aid.

I squeeze my eyes shut for a second, like that might make it hurt less. Spoiler: it doesn't. When I finally tap it open, my chest caves in on itself.

Gia,

I don't even know where to start. There's an ocean between us and it feels like it's ripping my chest open.

I can't take back what I said. I can't take back how selfish it was to ask you to stay when I knew you deserved more. You deserved everything. And all I ever did was take from you.

I didn't get over you then. I won't now. You're it for me. You always were.

I love you.

Uncontrollably. Eternally. Endlessly.

And so, I have to want your happiness more than my own. Even if it destroys me. Even if it means watching you live a life I'm not part of.

*I'm sorry. I'm sorry for every time I made
you doubt yourself. I'm sorry for every time
I wasn't enough. I'm sorry for all the ways I
broke you when all I ever wanted was to be
the one who held you together.*

*You deserve joy so big it scares you. You
deserve a love that doesn't come with
apologies and scars. You deserve a life
that doesn't have me dragging behind you,
weighing you down.*

*So if letting you go is what it takes—if
stepping back is the last good thing I can do
for you—then that's what I'm doing.*

I love you, G. In every world. In every lifetime.

Always have. Always will.

I hope you can forgive me.

Charlie.

The screen blurs. I blink hard, but it's no good. The
tears are already there, hot and furious. I drain the
prosecco in one go, ignoring the weird looks from the
happy couples spinning around on the dance floor.
Because how the hell am I supposed to sit here, sipping
bubbly, pretending my heart isn't shattering slowly.

I stare at the screen until the tears dry sticky on my
cheeks. Until the sun starts to dip low on the horizon,
painting everything in soft bruises of pink and orange.

Someone presses another glass of prosecco into my hand—or maybe I just take it. I don't even know anymore. I sip it mechanically, barely tasting the fizz, the sharpness.

I feel so lost. So broken. Like somebody scooped me out and left the shell behind.

All around me, the wedding party moves on without a care—laughter, music, champagne. A world still spinning when mine feels like it's stopped.

Then I hear it. The harpist starts playing a song so soft, so familiar it punches the air right out of my lungs.

I know this song. I know it in my bones. *Hear You Me*—the one I sang at Nico's funeral. The one I couldn't finish because the grief stole the words right out of my throat.

The glass slips from my hand and clatters against the table, sloshing prosecco everywhere.

Is this a sign? A message from Nico, telling me not to screw this up? Telling me I deserve to choose love—even when it terrifies me?

I wipe my face with the back of my hand, sniffling through the ache in my chest.

I swipe over to Instagram, thumb hovering above "Go Live," the harpist's soft notes threading through the Roman dusk. My heart is hammering, and I'm warm with prosecco, and everything feels too much and not enough all at once.

Fuck it.

I tap "Go Live."

"Hi," I say, waving a little, mascara smudged, the wedding lights twinkling behind me. "Um... so, I crashed a wedding in Rome." I laugh, shaky, but it bubbles out anyway. I can see people joining—little hearts flicker across the screen. It makes me want to run, but I stay. "I know I joke around a lot on here," I say, voice catching, "but I... I want to be serious for a second." I take a breath, eyes flicking away from the camera, grounding myself in the soft melody of the harp. "My brother, Nico, died a long time ago. I don't talk about it much. But this song..." I gesture toward the harpist, who is still playing, the notes carrying into the evening air, soft and familiar like an old bruise. "It's called Hear You Me," I say. "I tried to sing it at his funeral, but I couldn't finish. I just... couldn't."

My throat is tight, but I push the words out because they matter.

"And I don't know, maybe it's the prosecco talking, or the fact that I'm here in Rome, or the way the light is hitting everything, but I... I want to finish it. I need to finish it. Even if it's messy."

My hands shake as I lift my glass toward the camera, my reflection wobbly in the fizz.

"Here's to starting things we could never finish," I whisper.

And then, quietly, I let the words come, voice trembling, heart wide open.

I sing for me. For Charlie. For Nico.

For every jagged edge I tried to smooth over. For the love and loss I thought I'd buried. For the parts of me I've hidden away, too scared to let them be seen.

I pour every ounce of myself into the chorus—every heartbreak, every hope that's still flickering inside me.

This is it. Me, finally showing up for myself.

My voice cracks on the last note, but I let it.

Because it's real. It's raw. It's everything I never said.

I lower the glass, tears hot on my cheeks, but I'm smiling.

"Anyway," I say, brushing a tear away, "that's all. Love you guys."

I end the live before I can take it back, setting the phone down with trembling fingers, the harpist's notes echoing in the warm Roman air.

And for the first time in forever, I feel like I can breathe.

35

CHARLIE

The Great Escape

I sit in the crowded departure lounge, hunched over my knees, my passport digging into my palm. The gate's open. People are lining up.

I should feel... something. Relief? Closure?

I don't.

My body's here, but my heart's somewhere in Rome.

The final boarding call crackles overhead. They're starting to herd the last few people onto the plane. I should get up. Move. Start over. Run, like I always do.

I pull out my phone for the hundredth time. Nothing. No messages. No missed calls.

I stare at her name on the screen until the letters blur.

For a second, I think about letting it go. Letting *her* go. Telling myself it's what she deserves—freedom from me, from all the ways I've failed her.

But the truth is, she deserves better than the mess I left her with. She deserves an apology. She deserves someone who shows up, even when it's hard. Someone who fights for her, the way she's fought through everything else in her life.

Someone who doesn't run when it matters most.

I take a breath. Then another. My pulse roars in my ears, but for the first time in a long time, I feel clear.

I scroll to her Instagram, the last live still sitting at the top of her stories. I watch it—her voice cracking as she sings, mascara smudged, laughing and crying under twinkling lights. Brave. Messy. Alive.

God, I love her.

I don't deserve her, but I'm done letting that stop me.

The gate agent makes the final call for boarding, but I don't move. I don't look at the plane waiting outside the window. Instead, I stand, sling my backpack over my shoulder, and walk straight past the gate.

My phone is in my hand before I know it, fingers moving fast as I pull up a new search:

Flights to Rome.

I don't care what it costs. I don't care how messy it is. I don't care if she tells me to go to hell when I get there.

She deserves to hear me say I'm sorry, to hear me say I love her, to see me standing in front of her instead of hiding behind a screen or a plane ticket out of her life.

This time, I'm not leaving.

Not without a fight.

36

GIA

First Day of My Life

The espresso is bitter, clearing the fuzz from my head as the hotel lobby hums around me. My phone lies face down, the screen dark, and for once, there's no urge to reach for it. Not yet.

I drain the last of the cup, drop a few coins on the saucer, and stand.

Outside, Rome is alive. Warm, gold-lit, pulsing with possibility. I step into it, letting the air sober me, letting the city swallow me whole.

I walk without thinking, letting my feet guide me through winding streets and lantern-lit piazzas, the hush of the late hour pressing soft against my skin. The last of the wedding laughter still clings to me, the harpist's song echoing in my chest.

Rome unfolds around me, street by street, as I walk. Until finally, I find myself standing in front of it.

The Trevi Fountain, glowing graceful and delicate, heart-stopping under the Roman sky, water rushing and folding over itself in silver sheets. People mill around, tossing coins, taking pictures, whispering wishes into the dark.

I stand there, taking it all in. Letting it *be* enough.

I don't toss a coin. I don't make a wish. For the first time, I don't need to.

Instead, I find a spot near the edge and sit, the marble cool beneath my palms. I close my eyes, breathing in the scent of wet stone and the faint sweetness of a nearby gelato cart.

It's peaceful, in a way I don't think I've ever let myself feel. Like I've spent so long bracing for the next heartbreak, the next goodbye, that I've forgotten how to simply *be*.

I think of Nico. Of his laugh, of the way he used to drag me out for late-night drives just to get milkshakes and blast music until we felt alive again. I think of the song, of the words I finally let myself sing.

I think of Charlie.

My chest tightens, but I don't run from it. I let it sit there, heavy and honest.

I don't want to lose him. But I won't lose myself for him, either.

If he wants me, he knows where I am.

And if he doesn't—

I close my eyes, letting the rush of the water fill the spaces where fear used to live.

I'll still be here. *I'll still be me.*

And that's okay.

I press a palm to the cool marble and let out a slow, grounding breath.

"What did you wish for?"

The words cut through the rush of the fountain, warm and low, curling around me before I even turn.

My heart stutters.

I know that voice.

Hope and fear crash into me all at once, leaving me breathless, my pulse thrumming in my ears.

For a second, I think I'm imagining it.

But then I turn—and there he is.

Charlie.

Hair a mess, eyes tired, breath coming in sharp little bursts like he ran here.

Like he's been looking for me.

I blink, trying to be sure he's real. "What are you—"

"I didn't want to leave," he blurts, stepping closer, voice shaking. "I couldn't. I got to the gate, and I... I couldn't get on the plane, Gia."

I swallow, the marble cool under my palms, the fountain roaring behind me.

My heart is pounding so hard I'm sure he can see it, the air thick between us, everything I want and everything I'm afraid of standing right there.

He drags a hand through his hair, eyes never leaving mine. "I didn't know where to find you. I went to the hotel, someone said you might be here." He huffs out a breath, a broken laugh. "I was so fucking scared I'd be too late."

I stay quiet, letting him speak. Letting him try.

His jaw works, his eyes shining. "I've spent so long running—from everything, from you, from how I feel. I hurt you. I know that. I told myself you deserved better. But I can't pretend I don't love you. That I haven't loved you since the day you owned the pit and scared the shit out of me."

A laugh cracks out of me, tears welling.

Charlie takes a careful step closer. "I'm sorry," he says, voice low, rough. "For leaving. For staying away. For dropping it all on you before you left, like a coward, because I was too scared to let myself love you."

He drags a hand through his hair, eyes never leaving mine. "You are so damn easy to love, Gia, and I hate myself for what I did to you. For the choices I've made. I don't expect you to forgive me. But I need you to know that I'm done running. I want you. All of you. If you'll let me."

The world hushes, the fountain's roar softening to a pulse.

My heart stumbles, breath catching as his words settle in my chest. Part of me wants to believe him, but another part is still braced for the fall.

"You asked me what I wished for," I say quietly.

His eyes search mine, bracing.

"I didn't wish for anything," I say.

His face falls, and it cracks something in me.

"Because," I continue, "for the first time, I didn't feel like I needed to."

His eyes soften, his shoulders dropping as if he's letting go of something heavy. "Gia—"

"I'm not going to chase you, Charlie," I say, voice steady, even as my heart pounds. "I can't lose myself for you. Not again."

"I know." His voice cracks. "I'm not asking you to. I just…
I want to be someone worth staying for. I want to try. I
want to be the man you deserve, and I promise I'll stop at
nothing to prove it to you."

A pause. The city, the fountain, everything holding its
breath.

"I don't want to lose you either," I whisper

His eyes fly open, relief flooding them. "Okay," he
breathes, stepping closer, reaching for me, waiting.

I stand, meeting him halfway.

His hands cup my face, thumbs brushing away tears I
didn't even know had fallen.

My breath catches, a flicker of doubt fluttering in my
chest, but I lean into him anyway.

Then we're kissing.

And the world falls away, one breath at a time.

It's everything—relief, fear, longing, love. Years of
heartbreak and hope folding into this single moment
under Rome's magnificent glow.

When we break apart, breathless, he rests his forehead
against mine.

I laugh, tears threatening again. It's ridiculous,
cinematic, so cheesy I could scream.

But it's perfect. It's messy.

It's us.

"I love you, you know," I whisper, the words trembling
but true.

His breath catches, a soft, disbelieving smile breaking
across his face. "Yeah?"

"Yeah. Always."

I don't care if people are staring, or if it feels wildly
implausible.

Because this feels like the ending to the movie I didn't think we'd get.

"Still don't know what we are," I tease, because even now, I can't help myself.

Charlie brushes a strand of hair behind my ear, his touch gentle, grounding. "We're this," he says softly. "We're everything we never said."

His forehead rests against mine, our breaths mingling, the roar of the fountain softening around us.

For a moment, we just stand there, holding each other, letting the world move around us.

I close my eyes, feeling the weight I've carried for so long start to ease, replaced by something lighter. Something that feels like hope.

His thumb brushes across my cheek. "You okay?" he whispers.

I open my eyes, meeting his. "Yeah," I breathe. "I think I am."

He smiles, small and real, the kind that used to make my heart ache. Now, it just makes it full.

"Come on," he says softly. "Let's go get gelato or something."

I laugh, wiping at my cheeks. "That's your grand plan? Gelato?"

Charlie shrugs, grinning. "It's Rome. Feels right."

And it does.

I slip my hand into his, letting him lace our fingers together. Warm, steady. Grounded.

We walk away from the fountain, leaving the glow of the lights behind us, stepping into the dark, into whatever comes next.

And for the first time in forever, I'm not afraid.

Because we're here.
Because we're us.
And for now, that's enough.

37

CHARLIE

Such Great Heights

R ome glows gold under the streetlights as we walk back, gelato cups in hand, laughter still catching in the air between us.

Gia hasn't let go of my hand, and I don't think she plans to.

And I'm more than okay with that.

We share quiet looks as we walk, the city alive around us, but tonight, it's ours. She steals a spoonful of my gelato, pulling a face like she's just died and gone to gelato heaven, and I can't help but grin, feeling lighter than I have in years.

At her hotel, we take the stairs slowly, our shoulders brushing, letting the silence speak for us.

Her room is a beautiful mess—clothes draped over chairs, the bed unmade, a coffee cup on the windowsill, the scent of her shampoo and something warm that makes my chest ache.

She drops her bag and turns, eyes bright, smiling, and it's like feeling the sun in your bones after too long in the dark. Warm in a way that sticks. Makes you believe maybe you can survive this life after all.

She pulls me in by the front of my shirt before I can say a word. Her mouth finds mine, hot and hungry, like she's trying to make up for every second we lost.

Her fingers slip beneath my T-shirt, tugging it up and over my head. I step into her until her back hits the wall.

We've done this before—fast, desperate, like we were running out of time—but never like this. Not when we've finally stopped saying goodbye.

"Still mad at me?" I murmur against her throat, lips brushing that spot just beneath her jaw.

"Always," she breathes, and tugs on my waistband with a look that makes me dizzy.

"Good." I grin, pressing my forehead to hers. "Means you're still mine."

She laughs—breathless, burning—and then she moans, soft and sharp, as I lift her. Her legs wrap around my waist, and for a moment, there's nothing else.

No distance. No past.

Just us.

Right here. Right now.

Starting again.

38

GIA

Two Years Later

The cemetery's quiet this early.

Dew clings to the grass. The air smells like cut stems and last night's rain. I kneel beside Nico's headstone, brushing away fallen petals with the sleeve of Charlie's hoodie. It's too warm for it, but I still wear it.

Charlie doesn't say anything—he never does when he comes here. But I know he talks to Nico. I've caught him doing it when he thinks I'm not listening—just quiet little updates, the way he always used to. Like Nico's still on the other end, rolling his eyes but listening anyway. I think in a way, it's helped heal him.

He sets the coffees down—mine, then Nico's—and sinks into the grass beside me, close enough that our knees touch. I glance at him. He's staring straight ahead, jaw tight, like he's trying to be invisible. I know how much it still hurts to see his best friend in a grave, but he always shows up for me.

I curl my legs beneath me, settling into the silence.

"Hey," I say quietly. "It's been a while."

I pick up the second cup and take a sip before placing it gently at the base of the headstone.

"Not corner shop coffee this time. Charlie s turned me into a snob."

He huffs a small laugh beside me, eyes still forward. I reach for his hand, and he gives it to me instantly.

"Nico… we wanted you to be the first to know." My voice falters, but I push through it. Then I reach into my pocket and pull out a little photo—black and white, blurry, beautiful. I set it down next to the cup. "You're gonna be an uncle."

Charlie exhales beside me, shaky. I glance at him. His eyes are glassy, but he blinks it away before it can fall.

"I think it's a boy," I murmur. "Charlie thinks girl. Either way, we're keeping your name in there somewhere. Hope you're cool with that."

The wind stirs the trees, gentle and warm, and for a moment, I let myself believe he hears me. That he's nodding, laughing, saying something sarcastic and sweet.

I rest my head on Charlie's shoulder. He leans into it, resting his cheek against the top of my hair.

"I wish you'd been there," I whisper. "To see me walk down the aisle. To make fun of the band. Charlie cried during the vows, by the way. So pathetic." I glance at him, smiling. "It was perfect."

"Not ashamed," he mutters, squeezing my hand.

"You would've hated it," I smile. "Which means you would've loved it, secretly."

I don't even notice the tears until one hits the back of my hand. I don't wipe it away. It belongs here.

"We're okay," I say. "We're building something real. It's a little chaotic, but we're both doing good.

"We're off to Lisbon next week. Charlie's got a guest chef residency for a couple of months, and I'll be working on some content while he's in the kitchen. It's nice, y'know? Knowing we have a home here, but we get to go explore too. We're doing what we love, together. It feels like... the best of both worlds."

Charlie brings my hand to his lips and kisses my knuckles.

I glance at the photo of the new life growing inside me, and it feels bittersweet.

"I miss you," I say. "Every day."

And I love you. Always.

Then we both stand, and I realise that the grief that's shaped me no longer defines me. Losing my brother isn't a wound, it's part of my story.

Charlie kisses two fingers and presses them to the headstone. I do the same, fingers brushing his.

And as we walk back down the gravel path, sun rising behind us and something brand new blooming ahead, I swear I feel it—his warmth in my chest. Like sunlight in my bones.

Acknowledgements

To Sandy, Sarah, and Sam—my brilliant beta readers. Your insight, honesty, and unwavering support mean the world to me. This book wouldn't be what it is without you.

To my pastries—thank you for always being in my corner, cheering me on, and being my safe space. I love you all more than words.

A massive shoutout to Chelsea for absolutely *nailing* the cover. You brought this story to life in a way I couldn't have imagined, and I'm endlessly grateful for your talent and vision.

To everyone who's read, reviewed, recommended, or simply felt something because of this book—thank you. Your support means more than I can ever say.

And finally, to the music. You carried me through heartbreak and healing, the highs, the lows, and everything in between. You've always been my lifeline—my soundtrack. Thank you for holding space when I needed to cry, laugh, sing, grieve, dance, feel, or just *be*. I owe you everything.

About the Author

Sonia Palermo writes spicy contemporary, paranormal, and erotic romance. When she's not immersed in writing, she enjoys cosying up on the sofa with a cup of tea and indulging in a good horror or romance movie. A true beach lover, Sonia finds inspiration along the beautiful south coast of England, where she lives with her son.

Also by Sonia Palermo

Scream Baby Scream

Papillon

Hot Girl Summer